Also by Ellis Sharp

## Novels

*The Dump*
*Unbelievable Things*
*Walthamstow Central*
*Intolerable Tongues*
*To Wetumpka*
*Lamees Najim*
*The Orwell Girl*
*Neglected Writer*

## Short Fiction

*The Aleppo Button*
*Lenin's Trousers*
(with Mac Daly) *Engels on Video*
*To Wanstonia*
*Driving My Baby Back Home*
*Aria Fritta*
*Quin Again and other stories*
*Dead Iraqis: Selected Short Stories*

## Non-Fiction

*Sharply Critical*

# WHAT VRONSKY DID NEXT

## Ellis Sharp

**Zoilus Press**

A Zoilus Press paperback
First published in Great Britain by Zoilus Press in 2021

A CIP catalogue record for this book is available from the British Library.

ISBN 9781838489809

Cover design by The Ever-Shifting Subject

Typeset by Electrograd


ZOILUS PRESS
York, England

WHAT VRONSKY DID NEXT

*for Louise*

SHE WAS TWENTY-TWO, thanks to her I'm on my way, interminable emptiness of the flat eastern plains, hour after hour of dull featureless brown farmland, she met him for the first time in Spain, she was his muse, his muse, his muse, Jan, Jan, Janine, so many echoes and connections – Gabrial, Gabriola! – and so in the echoing aftermath of a lost love and a huge fiction secreted from a shining absence I'm on my way, it's complicated complicated complicated, I am feeling *disassembled* she wrote, as though all my moves in life have been controlled by an invisible player even that I am but part of the dream of a restless sleeper, Jan had style, oh yes she had style, she wasn't the only one Louise, these human figures faint and insubstantial, was it one person only or were they all there? Malc retorted IN ANGUISH ABOUT EVERYTHING. HELP, LOVE YOU. S.O.S., I felt I'd swallowed a time bomb, Jan wrote later, much much later when everyone in this drama was dead, it can take decades to get at what happened, even then you encounter dark impenetrable corners, strange-shaped shadows, gaps, holes, a lanky spectral figure lurking one velvet late afternoon, a ruined church in Walberswick, the last Monday in July, so many parallel lives, mysteries, black holes, the rabbit-hole, Jan left from the Hotel Canada, the days of Pupdog and Rainbowpuss were over, there was she wrote *a woeful ending to our writing-paper love*, meanwhile the jet to this particular rabbit-hole continues on its long journey from Heathrow, I need something lightweight to fill these tubular hours, I combat the agricultural tedium below with the prose of a fresh paperback, curiously the English title amputates the first word of the American one, whose author's vengeful and needy second wife wrote a memoir subtitled *Scenes From My Life With Norman Mailer*, prefaced by the statement *All of the events in this book are recounted as I remember them, none have been invented, the dialogue, where not word-for-word, reflects my honest recollection of what occurred at the time,* I raise my second G & T to that ('Here's to what was'), the Wonderland Rockies a blessed relief after all that flatness, a strange name, Rockies, and look Louise (exclamation mark), now we are passing over Lake Okanagan – I like names with the letter 'k' in, one especially – the home of Wonderland's legendary Ogopogo, from this height it looks like you-know-where, a long straight slender black trench framed by steep-sided mountains, a pretty turn of phrase to be sure Louise, and I don't remember Okanagan at all, not now, not after all these years, it was background detail, that's what goes first unless you make notes, which on this occasion I didn't, and now the great silver airliner is moving high over the Tantalus range, the sun shines all the way across the land until five minutes before arrival, the great city invisible, buried under a dense layer of sea fog, we drop down into an all-encompassing greyness, *Sir, please fasten your seatbelt, we are landing in five minutes,* we plummet into the rabbit-hole, following the earlier arrival of John Buchan and the later departure of Elizabeth Smart, this place, this land of The Burning Hell, of a whiskey called No. 1 Hard, this land of big-eyed owlish raccoons with tails lopped-off for trophies found stuffed and mounted on bar walls, to get there in those days you needed a decent quantity of dosh, I was lucky back then, by the way did you know that in his lifetime Malcolm Lowry only published two novels (question mark), *Ultramarine* (1933), an interior monologue about a young man making a voyage as a seaman on a freighter headed for China, and his big book *Under the Volcano* (1947), a text which has never been much liked in Great Britain (from the most able to she that can but spell, there you are numbered), a novel which is highly regarded in Latin America and is a classic in Europe, over the years, on my travels, I've accumulated various editions, *Onder de vulkaan, Sotto il vulcano, Unter dem Vilkan, Bajo el volcán, Au-dessous du volcan,* books are useful objects, they can alert you to the strangeness of language, also useful for keeping out draughts, I'm L by the way, everyone calls me that, no one at all except complete strangers – those who don't know me at all – says Ellis, which was a mistake anyway, my mother, bless her, born in Dresden, sought to name me after her favourite American singer, but my father, a soft florid flabby Dubliner, had a twinkly fondness for the black deep restorative and, ach, the amber nectar, and to be sure on his way to the registry office did he not become just a wee bit confused, liquidly, in consequence of which his handwriting became alas aslant and spattery as a geriatric's, as foggy as that fog through which this jet is even now descending descending descending, and on the form he wrote not *Elvis*, at least not legibly, and so that third consonant became fixed for all time as an 'l' instead of a 'v', not that it made all that much difference in the long run as at school everyone called me 'Ell' which shortly became shortened, transforming me into 'L', and L it's been ever since, which I don't mind at all because it was late in the evening when K arrived, and if you can begin a novel like that, with a character like that, well, that was good enough for me, besides which L is also for Lowry, which brings me to why I'm here, falling through cloud and fog, in search of greater knowledge, to find out what made Malc tick, aesthetically speaking, because when Lowry died prematurely in a Sussex village in 1957 at the age of forty-seven he left a stash of unpublished manuscripts, therefore to understand what Malc the Alc was trying to do as a writer you really had to read the unseen stuff, and you must remember that back then Malcolm Lowry was almost entirely an enigma, there was only one biography, slick but at times empty, I hoped one day to write a better one myself, I never did, his life back then, much of it, was a murky mystery, begin with the manuscripts I thought and build from there I thought, and although I gave up reading (re-reading) him long ago, I shall always be grateful to Lowry and I will never regret his chronic and destructive addiction to the massive consumption of alcohol since thanks to the fruits of that epic excess, i.e. *Under the Volcano*, I met Irish Jack and Honey Lea and Milena, and although it is many many years since I've read that novel I will go back to it soon, I feel certain, empty words perhaps when there is only one certainty, a certainty which has a deplorable tendency to interrupt the flow, not least during a pandemic, yes, *Unter dem Vilkan* continues to inspire outside bleak narrow Great Britain, the French are keen, the Germans also have a soft spot, there are many homages, Latin America seems to love Lowry, lately let's not forget – let's single out for special mention (I would guess Thomas Bernhard was a massive influence) there's that Actes Sud text, which translated by Mandell (those last three letters!) reads: *Lowry the drunkard had definite need for a change of air, he joined the contingent of Anglo-Saxons who peopled the Zone, Joyce, Durrell, Hemingway, Pound the fascist and Burroughs the visionary,* Honey used to tell her friends that she and L were going to write a book together, what about? they'd inevitably ask and then she'd laugh and tell them while I flushed and said nothing, what larks, that's another unwritten never-to-be-written book, but I am getting ahead of myself, to begin at the beginning I couldn't get to the airport in time for my flight from North Farm House so on the platform of Havant railway station I say farewell to my mother (her eyes are moist with tears) and my father (I will send you, my only son, by airmail, once completed, the last chapter of my new manuscript) and I take an afternoon train to London and a coach to the airport from the coach station at Victoria, no Piccadilly Line extension in those days, in the next scene I arrive at the Centre Airport Hotel, Bath Road, Longford, Middlesex, *Adjacent to London Airport (Heathrow)*, it says in scarlet on the free notepaper in my room, which contains a Personalized Decca Executive Television, I discover on ITV there's a John Wayne movie, I select instead BBC2, a repeat, where Norman Mailer is being interviewed about his book on Marilyn Monroe, Norman Mailer is currently my number one man, writer-wise, yes, ma'am (we all have shameful secrets, Louise), I have *A Fire on the Moon* in my hand luggage, to read on the epic flight to Wonderland, on the way here I noticed there's a road that cuts the terminals in two, it's called Cromer Road, it makes me think of Cleo and the souring of our great love, the first draft had Cleo's mother in it, lately deleted, the pandemic and the desire for brevity put paid to her, Cleo is trembling with fury as a novelist would say, all things considered Cleo is quite a big girl, it's the big goodbye, yes, let's skip the grey, clogged details, I went back to North Farm House, a mock-Tudor converted farmhouse stranded amid sold-off fields converted from arable crops to bungalows, Bungalow-Land I called it, the quintessence of *Daily Mail* and *Telegraph* land, my punishment a brief dismal sojourn with the parentals, my mother was waiting with scampi and chips on a big oval plate, take a look at this L, my father said, holding out his work-in-progress, it was entitled 'Metal Bending' and was about Alpha-waves, Beta-waves, Theta-waves, and Delta-waves (no, me neither) but when Smorg was present, for so I called him, enlightenment was but a moment away, Alpha-waves, my father explained with all the lucidity of the blissed-out possessor of Ultimate Truth, are created by transcendental meditation, Beta waves are generated by conscious mental effort, Theta waves and Delta waves come with deep sleep, these waves originate in the limbic system, the old animal-brain lying beneath the

11

neo-cortex, Smorg licks his lips, strokes his nose, upends a tumbler of the grand stuff, no wonder I became interested in Lowry, the Rosenheim case, he continues, investigated by Professor Bender, my interest is starting to fade, is interesting, he insists, I am not myself convinced, interesting in showing how a young woman's waves affected whole electrical systems and telephones, moreover she was quite unconscious of being the agent, in others with more concentrated powers even a look is sufficient to bend metal, for example a spoon, Manning actually reports he once registered a thought on a tape-recorder when he was under stress, after a dozen replays the message vanished, Smorg sinks back, beaming, his evidence beyond all doubt, this reminds Smorg of Uri Geller, who states that his tapes vanish or that messages become obliterated, Smorg knocks back another bottle, a pint of plain is your only man he winks, I hand the manuscript back the next day, pretending to have read all sixty-eight pages, thank you, father, most interesting, I'm expanding it into a book, Smorg confides, his smile is serene, he is certain of complete success, I went to bed, I woke, the big day came, in those days boarding a jet aircraft was a cultural experience, in the boarding area there was a portrait of a tousle-haired man with long sideburns, helpfully identified underneath as *Robert Burns the Scottish bard*, a jet with a poet on the side, truly my early life was lived in a golden age, this was before the age of cheap flights I should add, everything about flight was in this era magical, plus this was my first trans-Atlantic flight, at this moment in the history of civilisation emissions meant only what lusty men experienced while asleep Louise and dreaming of Julie Christie, climate catastrophysics were as remote and invisible as a black meteorite tumbling ineluctably towards planet earth in the cold dark void of outer space, whereas now the forests are burning, the seas are rising, and not even scowling Greta and a classic novel can save us, in fact a fine literary style and fiction is useless wouldn't you say? at best a narcotic, a palliative, crime outsells litfic, readers want pace, suspense, sensible readable prose, engaging characters, a mystery within a mystery, and then at the end everything straightened out, wrapped up, explained, leaving the reader with the glow of satisfaction that comes after a delightful three-course dinner at a restaurant highly recommended by that Irishwoman who used to write for the *Guardian* before she defected to the *Sunday Times*, after all no one wants acid indigestion, do they? no one wants axes and ice and all that nonsense, I am straying off the point, it was a ten-hour flight, I was given a window-seat in a 9-seat row, lucky me, the L District drifted by below, absurdly small, and then an insignificant speck upon the landscape lacking the shadow that would one day fall terribly upon it and render it famous, another L, L for Lockerbie, and then the Outer Hebrides, but though my heart's in the Highlands I didn't recognise any of the islands, later, Greenland, expanses of volcanic rock, snow and icebergs, strange unidentifiable islands with isolated settlements and only one road, the ocean next, dullness continuing, then at last land, with glowing hearts we see thee rise, Wonderland! yet from this height it seems vast, flat and boring, perforated with tens of thousands of tiny lakes, there's a 30-minute stopover at Edmonton, it seems strangely small and reminds me of the town in *High Plains Drifter*, a movie which has not aged well Louise in its representation of women, and then at last the mighty gulf, it was late in the afternoon when L arrived in foggy Vancouver, I took a cab from the airport and the driver dropped me at the Austin Motor Hotel, 1221 Granville Street, Vancouver 2, the lower is the true Granville, architecturally it looked just like the Texas Book Depository, from which Lee Harvey Oswald shot President Kennedy, my room on the fourth floor

13

was immense and gloomy, the walls were faecal brown, the bed was a double, beside it was a gigantic mirror, there were no en-suites in those days but the room did have a basin, that evening I dined in the hotel restaurant, a rather bleak affair involving lots of plastic and no homely fishermen's tackle on the walls, I was horrified to discover that because it was a Sunday I was not permitted to purchase alcohol in this city, not even with a meal in a restaurant in a hotel where the diner was staying, Jesus, I felt a sudden piercing empathy with Malcolm Lowry's disgust at the petty restrictions of Vancouver, which I was now learning had endured long after his death, I wondered why he had even ended up in such a place (or rather just outside it), I assumed it was because his second wife, Margerie, was Californian, she either didn't want to move too far from her family – I knew of a sister – or because she couldn't bear to detach herself from a life beside the Pacific Ocean, after a dry supper I went to bed, I slipped, jet-lagged, into a deep sleep, voices screamed in the corridor outside my room but that night they were simply shadows drifting through heavy, dark dreams of Cleo, later I discovered I was residing in an institution popular with whores, addicts, drunks and strangers unversed in Vancouver, no wonder the taxi driver had assured me this was an admirable place for a first-time visitor to stay, conveniently situated for the city's strip clubs and tattoo parlours, the days here had a certain routine, during the day tramps poked around in the trashcans at the rear of the building, as dusk fell whores began to gather and loiter in doorways of the buildings on the surrounding streets, in the early hours people staggered along the hotel corridors, shouting and arguing and cursing, sometimes there were nocturnal surges of vomit across the grey threadbare corridor carpet, yes Louise, this hotel had atmosphere, it was like being in an American lowlife realist novel of the 1960s, exclamation mark, and it was cheap, next day when I went out I found the street strewn with broken glass and cops standing in groups on the sidewalk, I stared at their polished holsters, it was all very different to Norwich, yes ma'am, I'm a stranger in a strange land, where the streets have no name, well that's not entirely true but a lot don't, and the signs, the signs! on West 10th Avenue there's a restaurant with the message: HAPPINESS IS A SPLIT AND A SPOON, I need to blend, I buy maple-leaf scrubbies and a denim jacket, I wear sunglasses, now, gratifyingly, people start to stop me in the street and ask for directions, search me, no use asking L, I too am lost, no more than a miserable urban explorer, I start by going to look for the places where Malcolm Lowry lived in Vancouver, discovering that his last address – *the last address* – is just 150 yards around the corner, The Caroline Court Apartments, 1058 Nelson Street, on this bright day in August it lingers on every bit as desolate as Lowry described it, next to it is a ramshackle tin hut with a battered Union Jack metal flag attached to it, a sign reads WE SPECIALIZE IN BRITISH CARS, about fifteen minutes walk away the tiny wooden hotel at 1359 Davie Street still stands, it's a ramshackle structure clinging on against the twentieth century, the convent opposite has only recently been demolished but the haunted house with the tall chimneys is still there, his third address, which was his second address, on Gilford Street, is gone, now a skyscraper occupies the site, it was a long hot sultry summer that year, or so I remember it, but one strangely with frequent downpours of rain and sudden big rolling cold surges of mist along the downtown boulevards, the sunshine coast, yes that is how they try to market British Columbia, in fact it rains a lot, Vancouver is washed by dense sea fogs, which swell up when the warm air off the Pacific surges down the estuary and meets the snow-covered mountains which overlook the city, Emily Carr, you

15

won't have heard of her, a minor nineteenth-century Canadian writer and painter, said British Columbia was the wettest place on earth, but then she'd never been to the Highlands of Scotland, I was young, I was male, I was not remotely pansexual, the songs on the radio were 'Sweet Home Alabama' and 'See the Sky About to Rain', in the hotel bar I met Irish Jack who saw me reading *Malcolm Lowry: Selected Poems* and came and sat next to me, a terrific writer he said in Irish-accented English, his accent resembled Smorg's, at first I was afraid Jack might be a homosexual but I soon learned he was freshly separated from his Wonderland wife, so obviously he couldn't be That Way Inclined, we became great friends, I get to know the city, I go drinking with Jack, I am having one hell of a good time Louise, a morose editorial in the *Vancouver Sun* suggests that the city in which these adventures take place is *the lunatic asylum of the universe*, hell yes! I ride the silver buses which will take you just about anywhere in Vancouver for 25 cents, a sign says 4-WAY STREET just like the Crosby, Stills, Nash & Young LP and one day the bus I'm riding passes a house on fire and fire is a motif in *October Ferry to Gabriola*, in the novel the ferry turns back because a passenger is bleeding profusely from a tooth extraction in Vancouver, there's a reference to Shaugnessy Hospital, I had to go there to get my teeth fixed, an emergency, an abscess with lurid pain, I remember the dentist was in a foul mood and shouted at his assistant, one day I spot from the bus a Cadillac with an orange bumper sticker STOP POLLUTION – SHOOT A HIPPY and everyone round here sure has one hell of a sense of humour, the *Sun* headlines the tale of the year-long medical treatment of two children hideously burned in a fire OF HUMAN BANDAGE, when I told D'eath he replied that just before he'd left the city the newspaper had a photograph of two young boys in a Vietnam street one with his legs blown off and the other with his face napalmed, the headline was GRINNING LITTLE BEGGARS, the silver buses take me to Special Collections, it occupies the top floor, the fat librarian tells me with obvious pride that they have the manuscript of *Tarantula*, I'm not interested in *that*, I am granted a carrel – a small private booth with a door, a desk, a chair – I get one by a window, there are eight carrels in all, in two rows of four, my number is carrel 867, the collection is overwhelming, box after box of his manuscripts, thousands of pages of typescript, many annotated, Lowry was a great reviser, he wrote in pencil, in a tiny hand, insertions, tens of thousands of small revisions, changed words, additional sentences, they float in and around the lines of typescript like scores of distended balloons, trapped amid a grid of machinery, and here are all his abandoned works-in-progress, *Lunar Caustic* – a novella published by Jonathan Cape in a slim green paperback – is a mash-up of *The Last Address* and *Swinging the Maelstrom* and *Dark as the Grave Wherein My Friend is Laid* is here in multiple versions ditto *October Ferry to Gabriola* plus letters and photographs and an old Mexican menu and other such miscellanea, I discover that after publication of *Under the Volcano* Lowry applied for a Canada Fellowship and was rejected on the grounds that this was an insufficient achievement to merit such an award, I read the unpublished manuscript of the Nineteen-Thirties text which became part of the mutilated posthumous *Lunar Caustic*, the hero – who is plainly, almost transparently, Malcolm Lowry – refers to Charlotte Haldane, widow of J. B. S. Haldane, the famous scientist: To stick her finger up her arse it was her daily wont / And to her friends at Christmas she gave each one her cwont [*sic*], still the undergraduate at heart then, as for me I am somewhat miserable and lonely, I feel strangely isolated Louise, in a manuscript I find Lowry has written: My mid-life crisis began when I was five years old, and browsing among the stacks in the library basement – the library has a young librarian, a student, I call her Greensleeves – I come across a copy of *Travelling*, a volume of poems by Michael Hamburger, I think they are terrific, especially 'Zombie's Notebook': *September evening. Street after street the station of a long undoing...* and I pick up a copy of the Toronto *Star* at a news outlet downtown, I want to read its exclusive interview with Leonard Cohen, he is promoting his new album, *New Skin for the Old Ceremony*, Cohen says he is angry what the record company did to the cover, instead of using the medieval engraving of a copulating couple they substituted a monochrome image of the singer, it is not a good photograph, You get tired of getting kicked around by the latest guru and the latest revolutionary hero, he snaps, he says his fingernails are crumbling under the friction of the guitar strings, This time I'm in is now, this age of forty, this season of winter, he says, the *Star* identifies him as an ex-Boy Scout *and generally eccentric musician*, I need to move out of this hotel, I need to get a room somewhere in the suburbs, nearer to Special C, I have to buy a record player and get the new Cohen album, I need some music in my life, I have a buddy now but Irish Jack is someone who is not good for me, I need a woman friend instead, I hang out for a while with my lady Greensleeves, let's skip those soft starlit nights, her flawless young skin and elegance did not match what flowed from that orifice enclosed by sweet wet lips, expressions like *pick my ass*, I remember – but never mind what I remember – let's say she gave me rides but in the end I walked, I bought the paperback of *Marilyn* by Norman Mailer, *The $20 Super Bestseller Complete with Color Pictures Now Only at $2.50!*, Irish Jack is sinking and if I'm not careful he'll drag me down with him, Jack is into alcohol, drugs and literature, he was busted at fifteen for dope possession, at seventeen he was arrested for being drunk and disorderly, he tells me that when he was twenty he was hospitalised against his will, a mental institution, he believed he was the Messiah and because of this blessed identity he possessed the rare gift of being able to drive through red lights at 8omph invulnerable to the frailty of mere mortals, the traffic cops and the judge and the psychiatrist disagreed, he's through all that now, although recently while drunk he tried to trip up a man who was walking past, the fellow turned out to be a plain-clothes cop, Jack appears in court next month, he wants to be a novelist, also since breaking up with his wife he is in love with a girl named Mary, he explains she won't come across, you wouldn't believe it would you he says bitterly, Jack wrote Mary a long letter, pouring out his heart, he told he had masturbated two hundred times thinking of her, this courtship ploy alas doesn't seem to have worked, Mary told him he was disgusting and she never wanted to hear from him again, Jack's father has been in prison and is now in a home for incurable alcoholics, Irish Jack drinks whisky and smokes, cannabis mainly, he also devours amphetamines like candy, occasionally he samples cocaine, this is cutting-edge for the time, it costs ten dollars, the two of us go to the Commodore Cabaret on Granville to see Canned Heat it was either that or a movie, today the Eve cinema at 919 Granville is showing *The Tale of the Dean's Wife* ('The student body voted her THE MOST LIKELY TO...') with added feature *The Brazen Women of Balzac* ('Sex is not a sin. Not if you enjoy it!' – Balzac), from Thursday: *The Last Tango in Acapulco* ('The movie everyone's talking about'), *We take pleasure in announcing our selection to exhibit a film of unusual IMPORTANCE!* to wit *Erotic Dreams, A collage of private perversions and uninhibited diversions, SOON*, the Commodore is a vast ancient ballroom dimly lit with red bulbs, its ambiance is hellish and its clientele distinctly rough and seedy, years later when I saw *Twin Peaks: A Limited Event Series* I felt the shock of recognition, it's an enormous place with masses of chairs and tables grouped around a large dance floor, Jack and I retreat to a dark corner and hold our extremely expensive beers obtained from the rip-off bar, the band on the stage supplies massively amplified raucous rock, my eardrums prickle and ache at the volume, the band is too loud to assess quality – it's just a wall of noise, a thumping blurred Niagara torrent, the band plays for over an hour and I watch them under the illusion they are Canned Heat but they aren't, they are a warm-up act called Trix, Canned Heat finally come on very very late, I am astonished by how FAT the lead singer is, at this tawdry moment in my life I am a committed fattist I believe very strongly that a lead singer should be scarecrow-thin I am also at this time funda-mentalist in my musical tastes I really only like two sorts of music, one is singer-songwriter – Len, Joni, Neil, Cat, Bob, etcetera etcetera – the second is mainstream rock – Stones, Byrds, Chicago – but Canned Heat don't do that, they are a strange sort of electric boogie-woogie band, I don't like boogie-woogie, Jack buys some drugs from a man in the corridor outside the john and we split to a beer parlour down the road but the waiter refuses to serve us, saying that Jack doesn't look 21, Heck, he's actually twenty-five but waiters don't do rational debate, so we plunge on through the night and find a shabbier parlour full of knifed seating, where pale tired men sit alone, it has entertainment, a gyrating stripper, she is being avidly watched by a group of six older men, who cheer her on and whoop, when she has removed the last of her sequined clothing she simulates masturbation, rubbing her hand against her crotch, she slips her fingers inside herself, the whoops grow louder, finally she removes her hand and presses it against the noses of her admirers, who whoop some more and drop dollar bills at her toes, later we walk past brightly lit doorways where attractive-looking whores call out to us, hey says Jack, let's get us some kitten, I decline, Jack stops to talk to one, I say goodbye, which is all we ever say in life n'est-ce pas Louise? and I go on back to the hotel, where I drink from a litre bottle of Burgon Rouge and glance at the ads in the *Vancouver Sun, SPIRITUAL CHAPEL OF BROTHERLY LOVE Peter Pann Hall* – no typo – *1636 W. Broadway MR JIM GARVEY Clairvoyant Messages Refreshments Everyone Welcome*, at the end of that week I moved out of the hotel, I rented a room in a house on Larch Street, a long leafy street ten miles from Granville, the room was only available for six months but that was fine by me, built at the end of the nineteenth century, the house was the oldest one on the block, it was at the southern end of the street, where the house numbers were all in the five-thousand-plus range, an oak tree in the front garden was surrounded by open lawn, wooden steps rose to a porch with pillars which supported a small balcony above, the house was divided into three groups of residents, a young couple rented the ground floor, and upstairs was a living room with a small cooking area, a bathroom, and two bedrooms, nothing was separate, to get to my room upstairs I had to walk through the living room of the couple on the ground floor and up an open stairway, the house, just like me today, had seen better days, it creaked in the wind, the front door was impressive with panels bearing a design of carved roses, its top half had stained-glass panes with William Morris-style curling foliage involving leaves and birds but the green paint was curling away from the window frames and as you went up the steps to the porch they groaned and sank a little under each footstep, knots in the wooden stairs had dropped away, leaving dark holes, if you stood on the porch and looked down you could make out basement windows, smeared and opaque and half hidden under weeds, unlock the front door and step inside, there's a herringbone parquet floor which is shiny and emits a slight tingling odour of varnish, a big fireplace on the far side of a large living room, prepared for a fire with crumpled newspaper and heaped logs, a brass bucket containing more logs, big windows, through which sunlight pours, rubber plants in pots, a Lava lamp in which a large red amoeba slowly rises and gives birth, bookshelves with tall-spined art book, a writing desk and chair, a sofa, two easy chairs, a small television on stilts, freshly landed from Mars, you cross the room – Hi, Rick! Hi, Giselle! – Rick has a moustache at a time when few young men have moustaches, he is tall, slim, fit, about thirty, he is athletic, he is a physicist, his live-in girlfriend Giselle is a warm friendly brunette, she is French, she works at UBC as a secretary, though her English is perfect she speaks with a distinct husky French accent, L continues across the room and takes a flight of stairs to the right, which lead up to a wide living room, darker and more shadowy than the one below, this room lacks windows, the only light that comes in directly spills in from the door to the balcony, the top half of which has glass panels matching the front door, open this door and step out, you find yourself under the canopy of the oak tree in the front garden, its leaves rustle gently in the breeze, this is a quiet, tranquil neighbourhood of many trees and bushes, this is a golden time, the apartment has a poster of Ludwig van Beethoven by the fridge and a map of Middle Earth in the bathroom, the bookshelf in the living room has paperback copies of *The Favourite Game* and *Beautiful Losers*, two rooms lead off this upstairs living room, the one on the left is the bedroom of the other tenant, the one on the right is mine, the other tenant I have yet to meet, she hasn't moved in yet, all I'm told is that she is a woman with a dog, my room is big, perhaps thirty feet long, with a double bed facing a stained-glass window, below it lies a side alley with a rough surface, sometimes used by residents to drive along to park their cars at the rear of other properties on the block, the other side of the alley is the side of a timbered church, I like my new room, unlike the hotel room it is full of light, this neighbourhood is very quiet after Granville, I walk up tree-lined Larch to catch a bus to UBC on West 41st, if I take the bus downtown it goes past a huge sign: KITSILANO TRANSFER, a disused freight terminal where the Canadian Pacific locomotives have long since ceased to arrive and depart, and so the days go by, the air too is sweeter than fume-filled downtown, fragrances drift from colourful flowerbeds, velvety pungent roses bloom in the Pacific sunshine, I took a ferry to Victoria Island, in Nanaimo I visited The Bastion, they'd moved it from where it was in Lowry's day, now it is framed by the Salvation Army Thrift Store, the Bastion Realty Co., and a hut advertising ECKANKAR, THE PATH OF TOTAL AWARENESS, the Union Jack inside the Bastion is hung upside down, the tourist counsellor has never heard of *October Ferry to Gabriola*, the ferry passes Gabriola on the Vancouver route, it's just a small island, nothing remarkable, and so back to the mainland, in box 12 folder 10 I come across Lowry's record of a moment of inebriation: *I'm slightly drunk, though in a new way*, I come across Henry Aldrich's poem 'Five Reasons for Drinking', I discover there's a liquor store nearby on W. 41st, returning on a silver bus I drop by and carry home a twelve-pack of what passes for beer in this part of our spinning planet, the wall in my bedroom ticks in the summer heat, I have a white alarm clock, the late birds beat their wings loudly in the warm night, my new apartment buddy moved in one day when I was out, I didn't see her for a week, she left early in the mornings, when I was still asleep, I returned late when she'd gone to bed, finally, on a Saturday, we meet, hello, I'm L, I'm on a pilgrimage, I'm learning about

23

Malcolm Lowry, I'm consulting his papers at UBC, you've never heard of him, well, it's like this, I give her the quick version, she tells me her name is Honey Lea Maddox, she is twenty-three years old, her name is apt, she has a snub nose, honey-blonde hair, a tanned complexion, deep intense blue eyes, but my first impression is how prim and virginal she seems, she looks like someone whose father might be a priest, a good Christian girl, her long skirt goes down lower than her knees, she is dressed demurely in sensible clothes, she tells me she works as a clinical psychologist at Riverview Asylum, in her spare time she's studying for a Ph.D. in psychology, in the past she's worked as a nurse in the accident ward, she has terrifying anecdotes of people transformed into vegetables by minor head injuries, spinal injury frightens her even more, Honey (like Malcolm Lowry) is frightened of fire, she says the apartment needs a rope-ladder, without it we might be trapped, I say we could simply jump from the balcony on to the lawn, it's not far, I don't mind landing on grass, at worse a snapped rib or a fractured femur, she shakes her head, *spinal injury!* she replies, in trying to understand another person I always – if the opportunity arises – scrutinise the books on their shelves, Honey I discovered was into women, feminism, and liberation, with a dash of literary fashion, I spotted the spines – spines! – of Kate Millett, Herman Hesse, and Simone de Beauvoir, books with titles like *Woman Alone* and *The New Freedom*, eh moi Louise? by then I had finished the Penguin paperback of Iris Murdoch's *The Nice and the Good* and I was now reading a paperback by *the* hot new American writer, *Goodbye, Columbus*, Honey eats a lot of avocado, she introduces me to the fruit, I have never eaten an acocado before, years later, whenever I tuck into an avocado, I think affectionately of Honey Lea Maddox and wonder where she is, perhaps still hanging out with her shrink friends, she has two in particular, a thin bearded man and a fat woman, opposites attract, and a particular friend named Kevin, he is always dropping by, he is gawky, late twenties, and a bit odd, a vet, he never stays the night, a friend then, not a lover, no man ever stays the night, no lover, it seems, but then she looks like a virgin and dresses like one, after a further five days, indicating the heaped empty bottles in the bin by the fridge, she asks if I'm an alcoholic, I indignantly deny the charge, okay, sure, so I regularly bring back twelve-packs of beer, but the bottles are ridiculously tiny, the brand name is Toby, I am confident that this is not a tribute to Laurence Sterne, you have to drink four bottles of Toby to get somewhere close to a pint, what's more it's not beer at all, but weak, sweet lager, *Alkie* she says, unconvinced, *Get back*! this last remark is addressed to Briar, her red setter, to get the room she told Rick she only had one dog, but she was lying, she has two, the other one is called Nimba, also a setter, they are big, young lively dogs, but then so were we all back in those shining days were we not Louise, question mark, exclamation mark, one evening soon afterwards I went to the dollar-fifty movie theatre on West 10th, it showed old movies and that night the feature was *Five Easy Pieces*, at this moment in my life I found it electrifying, a cultured drifter (Jack Nicholson when he was thin, with hair) goes home to Washington State to visit his sick father, he's too embarrassed to take along his working-class waitress girlfriend, so he leaves her at a motel, back home he promptly falls into bed with his brother's attractive fiancée, at the end he abandons his girlfriend at a gas station and rides off into an unknown future, the soundtrack was stunning, apart from the piano pieces alluded to in the title – two by Chopin, one by Bach, two by Mozart – there were four songs by Tammy Wynette, including her two best-known ones, the strangely intense emotional impact that *Five Easy Pieces* made on me that night was such that I didn't want to watch the next feature (Charles Bronson revenge schlock), I left the cinema and walked the twenty-eight blocks back to the house on Larch Street, when I got there Honey was in our communal lounge with Kevin, as I came up the stairs and into the room I received a cheery greeting from Honey and a sullen nod from Kevin, Honey exuded warmth, Kevin only hostility, we chatted, she and I had a long conversation about movies, Kevin was acting weird, he picked up one of the kitchen knives, sometimes he jabbed it, as if making a debating point, the conversation continued, about music now, I did not like the way Kevin sometimes pointed the knife at me, he seemed strangely angry and aggressive, Honey tells me this house is haunted, the original owners both died of malnutrition within a week of each other, the bodies weren't found for weeks, really – question mark – I didn't know that, she says Rick told her, but maybe, I wonder, I think it possible, Rick invented this story, perhaps as revenge for her pretending she only had one dog, Honey insists it's true, just as I too insist this slender but not at all tall tale is true, a little twisted and warped and scorched perhaps but none the less real, no matter what the rot, the fraying of memory, the years piled on years until you start to shiver and shake and gasp for breath, no matter what the mosaic lure of patterning, it's a life sentence buster, Honey stands beside the throbbing refrigerator and she tells me she woke up the other morning and there was the bar of soap from the bathroom beside her bed, she has no idea how it got there, Kevin looks at me accusingly, even though never in my life have I taken a bar of soap from a bathroom and entered the bedroom of a stranger at dead of night to place it on her bedside table, he raises the knife, he pretends to aim it at me, like it's a rifle, he's nuts, jealous of sharing her perhaps, perhaps he can sense something, Kevin has known her for years, the tiny quiet unseen drip of Honey's honey perhaps, at this instant I recall once being alone in the house when a door suddenly slammed shut for no apparent reason, I tell them about Borley rectory, they've never heard of it or the poltergeist activity there, in the end I left them to it and went to bed, *What is a novel?* I discover that stale paltry question written in my notebook, the question goes unanswered, it is alongside other questions: what is an albatross doing on the library roof? am I drinking too much? what was the name of the play which the barman said he'd written and which would shortly be shown on CBC TV? who gave me that fistful of amphetamines which I swallowed? who doctored my drinks? why are the brewery workers on strike? who are those strange dwarfish figures in the darkness at the edge of my vision who chorus *soon there'll be only Uncle Ben's to drink*, why did I write: there are twelve hours in a jamjar? is this the twelve-pack talking? am I starting to turn into Malcolm Lowry? a cutting flutters out from a Dostoievsky paperback but it is not about the Russian, *Jack's return to normalcy begins with his moving his big toe, and this may be the best touch in the book, as he improves, he experimentally simulates intercourse with the mattress of his bed, under Mary's encouraging eye*, what the blue blistering blazes, question mark, Uncle Ben stares at me from the latest crimson twelve-pack, an ersatz Mother Gettle, suggestive in his bulky bearded way of an heroic round-the-world yachtsman who has found the secret of life in a homely retreat to the outback where on his farm surrounded by acre after acre of golden wind-rippled wheat he pursues the virtues of thrift and domesticity combined with the consumption of gallons of what purports to be beer, now I discover that the latest French and Italian editions of *October Ferry to Gabriola* delete October from the title, I am listening to Gordon Lightfoot singing 'That Same Old

Obsession', in the night one of the rubber trees in Rick and Giselle's living room crashes over and shatters, next it's Sunday morning, I watch *Agape* on TV, a religious programme, Bev carries a cardboard log over his shoulder and stops in a field to sing 'I'm Gonna Be Ready to Die', the compère says: 'Ask yourself, in all honesty, what are your values?' he quotes *Dostoievsky the Russian*, he speaks of Jesus in the desert *a long way from any groceries*, next: John Locke, who wrote: 'Life will see to it that you'll cry before you die', I see that Honey drives a white Nova, a big car, with many dents and scratches, it's done a mile or two, she asks me to put my record player in our shared living room, so she can play her LPs, she is a big Carly Simon fan, *Anticipation* is her favourite album, plus she is big on Joan Baez, she has *Come From The Shadows*, she keeps playing 'Myths', plus a lot of Hot Tuna, my own long-playing records that summer were *Captain Fantastic and the Brown Dirt Cowboy*, *Saint Dominic's Preview* and *Angel Clare*, yes ma'am, Proust had a cookie, Prufrock had his spoons, and L has a record collection to drag him back to the days gone by, and as Van has correctly noted we were oh so young and foolish then, one time not long after an event which will be described shortly we went downtown to see *Monty Python and the Search for the Holy Grail* with some of her shrink friends, English humour, it gets everywhere, on another day, also after the revelation which is waiting to reward the interested and attentive reader we went to see a Pink Panther film, the one where Peter Sellers makes a joke about a dog, the one with a slo-mo romp in a room full of drifting feathers, we were both afloat on joyous rippling sensation, a cocktail of valium and morphine which she'd filched from a cupboard at work, we went to a bar afterwards, the jukebox was playing an old Stones single, 'Long Long While', a song which haunts me to this day Louise, *Dear L*, Smorg writes, your mother and I are well, we both hope you are working hard, it may interest you to know that there has recently been a huge cover-up regarding sightings of three UFOs over Brighton, they were tracked on radar travelling at phenomenal speeds but the Ministry of Defence as usual is trying to conceal the truth, luckily there are some very bright people studying the matter, all the evidence suggests that the human race evolved somewhere else in the universe and was brought to our planet at a later date, do not believe all that nonsense by Darwin about evolution, Einstein was also wrong, he based his calculations on the observations of Morley and Michelson, who used crude instruments incapable of measuring with any precision, there is no doubt at all that the world is surrounded by an aura, i.e. the ether, because of this it has become obvious that we all need to rethink our outmoded conceptions of space, time and the cosmos, it is plain that human beings were once space travellers, this is because our planet was long ago visited by space travellers like ourselves (see Genesis, Chapter Six), your loving Father, P.S. I am writing a book entitled *Journeys into Inner Space*, I shall send you some extracts shortly, but please do not neglect your studies for them, your mother sends her love, I toss the letter in the bin, I spend day after day in my carrel in Special Collections on the top floor trying to make sense of Malcolm Lowry's career after publication of *Under the Volcano* in 1947, there is a mountain of manuscripts which are either unfinished or which existed in multiple overlapping versions, a couple have been licked into shape by his widow Margerie Bonner Lowry and Douglas Day who killed himself as did poor forgotten Conrad Knickerbocker who once asked William Burroughs why he started taking drugs, getting the reply: Well, I was just bored, Beckett just wants to go inward, first he was in a bottle and now he is in the mud, I am aimed in the other direction, outward; as I was saying *Lunar Caustic*, a novella, put out in a slim elegant paperback by Jonathan Cape, was terrific, *Dark as the Grave Wherein My Friend is Laid* wasn't, and later came *October Ferry to Gabriola*, these last two novels seem a crushing disappointment after the *Volcano*, Fabulous friendly feasible fearless fire-eating fate-defying far-fetched fir-fetching fucking fine rye, wrote Malcolm Lowry in the margins, about Vancouver whiskey, Special Collections, Box 20, folder 14, I write: Discussion of form in *Under the Volcano* largely involves a rehearsal of Lowry's defence of the manuscript in his long letter to Jonathan Cape of 2 January 1946, back then there really was a man called Jonathan Cape, who owned the publishing house that even to this day bears his name, plus back then the top man in the publishing house was actually prepared to engage in correspondence with a putative author, Cape's letter to Lowry, dated 29 November 1945, requested revisions to the text, since 'it would be a pity for it to go out as it stands, believing as we do that its favourable reception will be helped tremendously by the alterations', a reader's report urged that the manuscript be cut by a third or even a half, the reader found the opening chapters slow and tedious, he found the characterisation weak, he didn't like the flashbacks, the theme of alcoholism was too reminiscent of the recent smash hit novel and movie about a drunk, *The Lost Weekend*, Lowry's hero's hallucinatory inner life was too long, it was wayward, *wayward*, an interesting word, from the Middle English 'awayward', meaning 'turned away', in modern English: unpredictable and hard to control, and who was Cape's reader? he was William Charles Franklyn Plomer, C.B.E. (1903-1973) who having failed as a poet and as a novelist became a literary editor for Faber and chief reader to Jonathan Cape, his great discovery was Ian Fleming, who later dedicated *Goldfinger* to Plomer, luckily

Lowry told Cape in the nicest way possible what to do with his reader's report, either publish the manuscript as it is or just fuck off, Cape crumbled and the rest, yawn, is History, meanwhile in the daytime during this summer I mostly immersed myself in the manuscripts of *October Ferry to Gabriola*, I discover it was originally conceived in the form of three gigantic sections before it was cut down to size and broken up into short chapters with titles which seem inept or misleading, another Saturday rolls round, I offer to cook a meal for the two of us, Honey thinks that's a great idea, she offers to drive me to the Safeway supermarket in her white car, a stir-fry, beansprouts, sliced vegetables, avocado to begin, a bottle of wine, we sit facing each other at the small round table in the living room, Hey, you are quite a cook, she says, Not really, we eat, talk, drink, laugh, I forget what we were discussing, tickling and laughter, perhaps, shrinks are very hot on laughter and jokes and Freud, suddenly she's gone from her chair and she's sitting cross-legged on the carpet, Eh? tickle my toe, she says, she's wearing sandals, it can be achieved, I bend down, I tickle her toe, she writhes and giggles, she is not wearing a bra under that crisp white blouse, her left breast flops out, big and bouncy, we wrestle sportively, she comes almost at once, in great gulping moans of etcetera, then to my bed for a repeat performance, sleep, drowsy caresses in the morning, another game of tick-tack, at pillow talk time she tells me she hasn't had sex for a year, bless you Malcolm Lowry, next day was a Sunday, she left me (can you imagine this, Louise?) with her dogs, I listened to her Carly Simon albums, while she went climbing in Wonderland with a female friend, I wasn't invited, I was warming up some Heinz tomato soup for my lunch when Rick came upstairs to complain about noise, he wanted me to lower the volume on the record player, sure, no problem, he still looked uneasy, finally he said in a low voice that was

31

almost a whisper: It's nothing to do with me what you guys do upstairs but please don't do it in the living room, it's so *noisy*, it upsets Giselle, okay, sure thing Rick, Honey came back late afternoon, I don't *know* you, she said, she was no theologian, I found it an oddly shocking remark, she added: But I'll sleep with you again tonight, however, I have to leave early, work, okay, sure, there's a fireworks display in English Bay that evening, let's go, she says, so we went in her Nova, it was a Sunday in July, it was a warm sultry Pacific evening, the fireworks crackled and broke across a darkening sky, very pretty, exactly four hundred years earlier William Shakespeare was watching fireworks too, later I join Honey in the bath, we face each other, I soap her breasts, her belly, and then to my bed with its green sheets, *Must retain a minimal vocabulary, and mustn't forget to put on clothes, till it's time to take them off, When bodies couple, so do ambitions and self-conceits, The copulation of words*, Michael Hamburger wrote that, Monday, she returns after work, she comes to my bed again, but the next morning she said she's decided she won't sleep with me any more, she went back to her room to dress, that evening she didn't come back at the usual time, I sat in the living room, drinking bottle after bottle of beer, finally I heard footsteps coming up to the porch, the front door being unlocked, it was her, I've changed my mind, she said, as she crossed the room, she bent down and kissed me, said coolly I want to fuck, we talked and touched and eventually went to her room, the two dogs watched with interest and wagged their tails in amiable solidarity as she rode me, she had a freckled snub nose and big firm thighs, and so it went on, some nights she wouldn't, other nights she would, mind games, one evening we fuck twice, then she says she wants to go back to her room and sleep alone, fine, but at eleven she opens the door to my room, she's naked, she gets into bed, she strokes me until I'm erect, that doesn't take long, then she laughs and jumps out of bed and runs back to her room, I pursue her, get out of my room! she shrieks, what do women want? Freud puzzled over this and never came up with much thought Erica Jong, I go back to bed and read Shakespeare's Sonnet 147, the phone rings in her room, she shouts: It's for you, long distance, an old friend, Godawful timing, but I can't talk, not with Honey glaring at me, I terminate the conversation, come to bed she says, you're treating me like shit I reply, oh fuck off, she retorts, I go back to my room, she leaves for work at 8.30am without a word, Honey was a feminist, she liked to be on top, she had the rare ability to experience vaginal orgasms, simply by mounting me and moving herself to and fro according to her own rhythms, all I did was lightly stroke her beautiful bottom and run my tongue against her swinging breasts, please, no more of this, this is pure Henry Miller, her breasts refuse to stay hidden, they had a saddle of freckles, sun-kissed, I had staying power in those days, spare us L, please, no more, too much information, change the fucking subject, okay, let's avert our eyes, let's examine the CERTIFIED COPY OF AN ENTRY OF DEATH, price 3s. 9d., REGISTRATION DISTRICT Hailsham, a Sub-district of the County of East Sussex, the death occurring on 27th June 1957, the Occupation of the deceased: A Writer; the Cause of death: (1a) Inhalation of Stomach Contents (b) Barbiturate Poisoning (2) Excessive Consumption of Alcohol, Chronic Alcoholism, Swallowing a number of barbiturate Tablets whilst under the influence of Alcohol, Misadventure; it's around this time I write to Margerie Bonner Lowry down in California asking her what happened to Lowry's essay 'Halt! I protest!' and she writes back in a letter dated 10th August of that year: I had it, she explains, and I think after struggling with it for months trying to make something printable of it I threw it away as being too amorphic and undeveloped and long-winded to be readable, so, gone, she chucked it out, I am left with an absence, sometimes, to revert to that apartment, that summer, that blonde, sometimes during a lazy weekend afternoon fuck we'd hold a conversation while I rose and fell between her golden thighs, once, I remember, I accused her of penis envy, Yeah, I'm full of it, she said sceptically, You most certainly are, I winked, what larks, the next weekend we went to Wreck Beach, the nudist beach on the shore below a wooded section of the campus, we lay and sunbathed nude, at Riverview, she says, there's a patient who repeatedly goes up to the TV and masturbates over the screen, the nurses find it tiresome having to clean it, she speaks of the pleasure of showers and high-pressure hoses, among her few possessions is a big portable mirror, she laughs, we'll write a book together, a guide to techniques, and now it's a quiet Sunday afternoon, the service has finished in the church across the alley, the choir has stopped singing, Honey and I are in my bed, I hear a noise in the living room and then a cough, I get out of bed, naked, and slip on my dressing gown, I step out of my room, being careful to shut the door behind me, Kevin is standing there, I called by to see Honey he says, his face is white and his eyes are taut with suspicion, his eyes wander to my bedroom door, she went out, I say, I can hear the giveaway tremble in my leaden voice, how delightfully fictional this scene is, real yet unreal, Kevin's narrowed eyes roam around the room they focus on Honey's car keys which are lying there on the little round table 'I see' he says grimly but he doesn't he can't he only *suspects*, now his hand drops casually down, he has the cutlery drawer open, he has a knife in his hand, this is where I came in, he looks coldly angry, but then after an hour or so during which my overheated heart thuds and bubbles he at last puts it down and returns it to the drawer, he deflates and wrinkles and grows smaller and smaller and in silence he

34

slowly slowly goes back down the stairs, after Kevin had gone Honey and I fell asleep, then woke later and fucked, afterwards we watched *Room at the Top* on TV, I will always remember those final scenes in the movie, especially the child's toy car, the next evening Honey told me she'd been to see Kevin, she told him I was in bed with a girlfriend when he'd called, it wasn't her she swore, she said it had been embarrassing for me, did K believe her? I really have no idea, she lied so often did Honey, she was lustful, restless, indecisive, on impulse she decided she wanted to go to Alaska, a vacation, without me, without the dogs, she put them in kennels, I said I'd go with her as far as the ferry from Seattle, she said yes yes please come with me, I had to go to the American consulate in Vancouver to get a visitor's visa to enter the States, next day she drove us to Seattle, we stayed at the 6th Avenue Motor Hotel, after we checked in we ate a forgettable meal at a forgotten diner, then we headed for the hotel bar, it seemed to be full of silver-haired men with young women, hookers Honey whispered, our hotel room had a big white screen on the wall, for showing porn movies she explained, she was tired after the long drive, as we went about our goodnight sedative an odd thing happened, she climaxed and I was almost there when her eyes tightened, she twisted her head and shrieked *Fuck Off!* at first I thought she meant me, I was perplexed, then I followed the line of her stare, I saw that two men had opened our bedroom door, they must have had a key, the taut silver door chain held them back, they stared in, grinning, then they ducked away, were gone, Honey pulled herself free, she ran across the room and slammed the door shut, next she dragged a chair and wedged it against the door handle, I said I'd phone reception, Honey shook her head: those guys are probably something to do with the hotel, we should just forget it, the hotel has our address, next morning we checked out, her ferry didn't leave until the evening, we did a few things, we drove to the Space Needle and went up in the elevator to the top while a guide showered us with statistics, I was more interested in my view of distant hazy Mount Rainier zone of modern myth! for it was over hazy there that in 1947 pilot Kenneth Arnold saw nine shiny UFOs flying in formation, they were convex in shape, slender, as big as a passenger aircraft, and flying at well over 1,000mph, that was the story, but that bright day nothing glinted around the mountain's peak, afterwards we descended and she drove to the shops downtown, later we went to a park for a walk, then a burger bar, where we ate burgers, salad and fries, Honey drove me to the Greyhound terminal for me to catch the bus back to Vancouver, I was wearing my Donald Duck T-shirt, we embraced and kissed and then we went our separate ways, while she was in Alaska I went out drinking with Irish Jack, who was always there in the background when I wanted to talk about literature or get drunk, Jack had managed to get hold of Frankie Trumbauer's recording of *For No Reason At All in C*, which Hugh Firmin mentions in *Under the Volcano*, I went back to Jack's current residence in a slum off Chinatown to hear it, three minutes and four seconds of jaunty jazzy music recorded in New York on 13 May 1927, the day Hugh sets sail for China, Lowry used music and literature to stitch together the lives of his characters and why not? while she's away I watch a lot of TV in the evenings I watch a bald figure named Mr Clean spring from a box and purge bourgeois households of stains Mr Clean hops smiling into lavatory bowls and departs leaving them twinkling and pure Louise, there's also a kid equally dedicated to the war on filth, he's a shambling neurotic youth who cleans stage floors during the interval at lightning speed, a fat laughing showbiz entrepreneur pats him on the back, stuffs a cigar in his shirt pocket and says he'll make a star of him, asks

What's your name, kid? *Johnson* jingle-jingle, yes, folks, you can't beat Johnsons' floor polish, she came back, I wasn't there at the time, but when I got back from Lowry's margins there was a big notice on her bedroom door KEEP OUT, she eventually emerged from her room, while I was drinking beer and reading a book, that summer after Dickens I had moved on to Dostoievsky I had reached – appropriately you might say – *The Idiot*, I was finding it hard to concentrate, I knew from the light beneath the door that she was in her room, plus there was a rumble of thunder outside and the distant flicker of lightning, the air was hot and full of electricity, it was going to rain soon, she emerged and stood before me, I've made a decision, she said, I am never sleeping with you again, we're through, I regret ever sleeping with you, okay, fine, sure, you said it, and just then, as in a cheap novel with a lurid jacket and the ejaculations of celebrity writers and corporate reviewers, the rain began, it started with a few slaps on the panes in the balcony door and slugs of water slithering down across the coloured glass and then the pattering increased and a moment later the rain was torrential, it hissed on the lawn below and in the branches of the billowing oak, you seduced me she said bitterly, I always get into messes like this, you plied me with beer and wine, you bewitched me with your talk of books and movies, you made me laugh, your soft English voice caught me in its net, no, surely, this dialogue is false, it's not true, I said thickly, you were the one who asked me to tickle your toes, you had it all planned she said, of course I didn't, that's garbage, she added sadly (I can still hear her voice): I would have liked you as a friend but now we can never be friends, there would always be that sex hanging in the air between us, it was time to move on, my lease was almost run, the room was wanted by another, final tip, she said, some sort of smile there perhaps, never fuck a psychologist, quite, it takes a couple of weeks for me to fix up new accommodation, Honey avoids the living room, she sits in her bedroom most of the time, she keeps the door closed, once, when she came out, I saw she'd changed the position of her bed, I sleep alone, I wake, I dress, I go out, I just miss the 41 bus, it usually gets me to Special Collections in fifteen minutes, so I take the next bus to Dunbar, transfer, wait ten minutes, catch a bus to Alma, just miss a 10 going west and wait fifteen minutes for the next number 10, I board, after a while I realise it's heading back downtown, apparently it's been re-routed, it's one of those days, I come back after a long day with Malcolm Lowry and she's listening to her LP of the soundtrack of *A Man and a Woman*, she seems bright and cheerful but I have nothing to say, you're sulking she says just because I won't fuck you, quite likely I suppose, I'm not in a conversational mood I reply, I go back out again and walk the streets, when I return she's sitting on the balcony, looking miserable, by the time I've unlocked the front door and gone upstairs she's gone back into her room, apart from Dickens and Dostoievsky my light reading also includes Shakespeare, I scrutinise my new copy of the Signet *Timon of Athens*, the Introduction asserts that the play is flawed because the Fool is not properly integrated into the action, I continue to ride the silver buses to Special Collections, I continue my voyage through the manuscripts, the handwriting in pencil, I read an early manuscript of his masterpiece, I discover that the vultures which float expectantly in the blue sky at the end of Chapter Eight originally flew at the end of Chapter One, that's the kind of frisson you get from reading manuscripts, you learn how authors rearrange their texts like jigsaw puzzles until the last piece is in place, you learn how the pattern could always have been different to the one that appears in the printed book, you learn that the best jigsaws are designed to have missing pieces, you learn that characters won't keep still, that the white clouds melt, that the puzzle rests on a surface which isn't flat, that the room has a slight vibration, that the wheel's still in spin, and off I went, I found a new room, not far away on West 41st, it was near enough for me to carry my stuff there on foot, half a dozen trips, Honey didn't offer to help me with her car, she stayed out of sight, like I was the bearer of an infectious disease, which plainly I wasn't, and neither was she, even though I'd never bothered to use a contraceptive, wild and dangerous sex was our connection, and see! as good ol' D. H. Lawrence said (you remember) we came through, unscathed, hygienic for a fresh start, I remember it with such sharp clarity Louise, that exit, I'd bought the LP of Vivaldi's *Four Seasons* in the fashionable new version with James Galway – Galway! – playing his flute, it became the soundtrack to my departure, I left the LP playing while I scampered in and out with my boxes, a week after I'd moved out there was a note pushed through my letterbox, *A parcel has arrived for you, please come and get it, H*, I wanted to see her again, perhaps she'd invite me in, perhaps she'd missed me, perhaps we'd go to her bed and it would be like old times again, how my heart thudded as I went out, turned right, then right again, but plainly she hadn't changed her mind, the parcel was lying in the porch, I picked it up and took it back to West 41st, I tore it open eagerly, then my face fell (eight storeys), it was the manuscript of Smorg's latest unpublishable book, let the camera track away from the typed sheets and into a darkness, it is night, it is the fall, it is raining hard, my new home is Apartment 4E, 2307 W.41st Street, Vancouver V6M 2A3, this is a small housing complex in back of a modest zone of shops strung out along W.41st between Larch and Balsam, a driveway between two shops leads to a residents' car park, there are five two-storey apartment blocks, with each storey divided into two apartments, each apartment has a living room, a kitchen, a bathroom and two bedrooms, I have a landlady who is sub-letting, she tells me her name is Alicia and she is an air stewardess, actually she's called Alice but I don't discover that for a while, this is after all Wonderland, Alicia is a single, older woman, a ripe thirty-two, she wears a great deal of make-up, she is slightly nervous of me, You're not a psycho are you? I assure her I'm not, I'm English I explain, I wear a tweed frock-coat, she tells me she's in a relationship with an Elvis impersonator in Hawaii, a place she jets off to frequently as a working girl, she shows me a photograph of him, a man running to seed in a tight-fitting white suit which looks like it might burst along the legs and across the stomach, Alicia owns two Siamese cats, vicious pests with deep Egyptian eyes filled with strange wisdom and malice and anger, she explains I'll need you to clean their crap and replace the litter in the tray when she's away, fine by me, Alicia sleeps in a four-poster bed, she has a glossy-magazine notion of style, the bed seems utterly incongruous in this modern apartment, her bedroom is a zoo – a zoo of soft toys, as if she was two years old, tortoises and penguins smile from shelves, pink elephants and yellow Teddy bears jostle for position, it was an animal world where every creature had enormous eyes and a big happy smile, caught in a rictus of perpetual delight, an infant's world, where all those murky adult themes – lust, jealousy, envy, possession – never intruded, beaming soft-skinned creatures which would never suffer toothache, or develop polyps, or menstruate, or feel an ache in their swollen testicles – because, of course, they lacked genitals, there is always an absence at the body's fork – a furry nothingness, Alicia drives an M.G. because it's a sexy car, she's divorced and smokes forty cigarettes a day, she reeks of heavy sweet perfumes and nicotine, she's also, quietly, a heavy drinker, gin mostly, she's terrified of death, she tells me how once her jet filled up with smoke and she had to appear calm and tell the passengers there was absolutely nothing to worry about, which of course there was – *the plane is burning and might crash and we'll all die!* – but the pilot got them down and all the fire engines which assembled hungrily at the side of the runway weren't, most of them, required, on the music front her taste is distinctly patchy, Alicia likes Andy Williams, John Denver and *Verdi's Greatest Hits*, when she sees my Richard Harris LP (which I only bought for 'MacArthur Park') she enthusiastically tells me she owns an LP of him reading Kahil Gibran's *The Prophet* and it's just so, so beautiful, her small bookshelf includes *The Collector's Encyclopaedia*, *The Guide to Good Wine*, Kahil Gibran's *The Secrets of the Heart*, and several copies of *Playgirl*, I have never seen *Playgirl* before, handsome tanned hunks with lots of gorilla hair recline on sofa and beds, exposing curly jet-black and chocolate-brown shampooed bush capping a limp half-tilted penis, she comes home when I'm sitting in the dark watching TV, she says it's bad for my eyes to sit in the dark like that, she turns the houselights up bright, she regularly brings me unused airline food, hot beef dips from the Seattle flight, the manager of the apartment complex is a man called Mr Nixon, he sits in his office and glares at me as I walk past, on my second day he asks if I live here, I say, yes, I do, with Alicia, he doesn't look pleased, from my new address the bus I ride to Lowry's leavings displays a destination board which reads: JOYCE, I'd been down the Rabbit-Hole for long enough for my mother to miss me, I decided to fly back for ten days, the dutiful son, plus I wanted to see some old friends, I duly went and then I returned, I am skipping those ten days, they contain fire and injury and pain and Melanie singing 'Ruby Tuesday' at the Royal Albert Hall and Tom Paxton singing 'The Last Thing on My Mind' at Fairfield Halls, let's jump to that Friday, at the Air Wonderland office in Regent Street I am told my flight to the Rabbit-Hole leaves at 1.05pm, when I arrive at Heathrow the woman at the Air Wonderland desk scowls and tells me it isn't scheduled to leave until 2.35pm, she grudgingly checks my suitcase in but advises me with a smile that all departures are currently delayed by fog, when I left Camden Town that morning the sun was shining brightly but at Heathrow visibility Louise is down to ten yards, I spend the next eight and half hours in a terminal building overflowing with impatient dissatisifed passengers, I fight my way around W. H. Smith, where I buy a paperback novel: Graham Greene's *The Honorary Consul*, I find a couple of square yards of aisle carpet and sit there, reading half of the book by the time the call comes for the departures lounge, it is announced that the scheduled jumbo jet has been replaced by a Douglas DC-8, which due to its inferior engine capacity will take two-and-a-half hours longer to reach its destination, night has fallen like the house of Usher, forgive the allusion, irresistible, the board reads AC 853 WAIT HERE and nothing happens, I read three more chapters, the person next to me is doing a crossword puzzle in Russian, finally red lights begin blinking on the board and there's a rush for the gate, tickets and passports are checked for the last time, then a long walk down the final tunnel which leads not to the plane but to a line of red coaches, passengers are to be driven out to the plane, which is sitting out there in the darkness, it is night all the way, I drink gin and tonic (cheers, Malc!) and finish *The Honorary Consul* and doze, we descend into the Rabbit-Hole, the plane taxies to the wrong place for disembarkation, it takes twenty minutes to sort out this problem, the pilot apologises, sorry folks! at the carrousel my suitcase is nowhere to be seen, I wait and wait and then go to a desk and fill in a form, then it emerges the case has been sent down the wrong chute, it is out there, on an otherwise empty machine, performing a lonely orbit in a vast deserted illuminated hall, outside it is still night, and pouring with rain, I get on the downtown coach, I ask if I can be dropped off at 41st Street, the surly driver says he doesn't do stops, odd, since when I went the other way, I caught the coach on 41st, Vancouver slides past, pools of darkness, shiny lights, the windows smeared and shimmering with rain, the junction with 41st Street whips past, at the same moment an attractive young woman heads up the aisle and asks the driver if he could drop her off at the next block, sure, he smiles, no problem, I grab my case and hurry to exit after her, it is still pouring with rain, I go to the bus stop, I've just missed the connection back to Arbutus and 41st, I stand on the sidewalk watching the rain pelt down, by this time I realise it is Saturday morning in England, my literary taste continues to evolve, I write in a notebook – oh dear, oh deary me – that *The Honorary Consul* is 'a minor masterpiece', I in my brittle lusty twenties applaud the novel's jaded ethics, I laconically note the name of the woman Greene dedicated the novel to, one of the main characters regards God as a kind of sinister suffering clown, the protagonist is a tired drunkard who has learned a style of survival, in part it involves consuming, hurrah, half a bottle of wine, those were my interpretations then, I have not read the novel since that year, but now, rediscovering these old perceptions, and thinking of everything that is to come, I think perhaps I should, I will, I must, now it is December, I buy cartons of egg nog and mix them with rum, Malcolm Lowry would be proud of me, Alicia is away most of the time, flying, or on vacation, Honolulu, Mexico, I feed her vicious staring infinitely wise cats and clean their litter tray, I buy Lou Reed's album, *Berlin*, it seems to match my desolate post-Honey mood, one night, how apt! there are ten earthquake tremors, mild ones, eight-and-a-half inches of snow fall, I like snow, I walk thirty-six blocks in the snow, nobody walks

43

in these suburbs but L, I like the solitude and the deep snow silence, my favourite track on *Berlin* is 'The Bed', I like the LP enough to buy two more Lou Reed albums: *Lou Reed* and *Transformer*, neither is as good as *Berlin*, what happened to *Berlin*? I lost it somewhere along life's way, sad face, I'm bored and depressed I write in a letter to an old friend, how trite, on with the work, over those falls, through those weeds, meantime ubiquitous adverts scream at me *Drink Canada Dry*, in honour of Malcolm Lowry I am doing my best to live up to that slogan, I go to the liquor store and stagger back, Honey's voice rises in a cold chamber of my mind, *Alkie*, I reckon it's time to quit, I'm bored by Malc's multiplicity of meandering manuscripts, his tiny pencil hand has started to seem like barbed wire, I have enough material, I decide I'll go back to England in February, in the huge library among the dark stacks I loiter by shelves of early sixteenth-century literature, I browse, I come across *A Mad World, My Masters*, when the library shuts I catch a bus back to W.41st, each night I drink myself to sleep, daytime I go for breaks, I hang out in the refectory, I drink gallons of coffee, I read a lot, *High Windows*, *The Cocktail Party*, *Enemies of Promise*, *The Treasure of the Sierra Madre*, *The Little Sister*, some evenings I watch TV, I watch Cher's show, her guest is David Essex, I am bored and restless, Irish Jack is faraway, behind bars so to speak, I go alone to the cinema to see *O Lucky Man!* it's a surreal dream I write in a letter to my English friend, a laconic vision of modern Britain, on his way to Scotland the hero suffers appalling experiences which drag him back to London, I sleep, I wake, the day passes, night arrives, I go for a two-hour walk through a rainy night, I drink the last of my duty-free gin, *Fools that will laugh on earth must weep in hell*, Christopher Marlowe wrote that, December arrives, in Special Collections I am now the only resident researcher, known to all the staff, the other carrells are occupied by researchers who come and go, spending at most a week there, but now someone has appeared in the carrell opposite mine, she has been there for over a week, a small slim dark-haired woman, through the square of glass in the door I can see her head, bowed over whatever is on the desk, it's three weeks before we actually meet face to face, her name is Militká Slabczynski – *mee-leet-car* – but I shall call her Milena, after Kafka's Milena (and there's a Czech angle too, see – you must, you must – the Milena of *Bad Timing*), M was originally born in Bohemia, though she came to Canada as a young woman, she's on the faculty, she knows Prague, she goes back there sometimes, she knows Kafka's grave, I explain what I'm up to with the Lowry papers, we keep meeting in the carrell corridor and she asks me to come for coffee with her, we talk about literature, books, manuscripts, next day she brings me some Austrian sweet-cake, two days later she suggests coffee again, how old is she? I have no idea, mid-to-late thirties? she is bright and bubbly, she laughs and smiles a lot, her face is browned by constant exposure to sunlight, she mentions she's a keen skier, she hillwalks, she snow-treks, she tells me she likes mountains and high places, in the mountains there you feel free, there are laughter-lines around her eyes, her hair is black with a few strands of silver, the strands are only noticeable when sunlight catches them, Milena is married, she mentions her husband frequently in conversation, Waclaw Slabczynski is a political philosopher, she is in awe of his accomplishments, he has a great intellect she says, a great mind, she mentions there's a Czech novel I really ought to read, from what I've said about my literary tastes she's sure I'll enjoy it, it's called *The Joke*, yes, that same month I was reading *High Windows*, it was only decades later that I learned that this was the very month when Larkin wrote 'When first we faced, and touching showed', a poem about two lovers and their first

45

physical encounters, two lovers who have had other loves and other bedmates in their pasts, a poem about a secret love, it was never published in Larkin's lifetime, a small, ticking timebomb left to explode in later years in the faces of those who thought they knew him best, secrets, everybody has them, don't they Louise, question mark, yes, December, bright bleak December, several coffees later Milena asks if I would edit a book she's writing, it's on drama, she'll give me $200 for my help, it's an offer I can't afford to refuse, my money has pretty much drained away on living expenses and my old friend Toby, she takes me to the Faculty Club and buys me lunch, she orders a bottle of wine, she tells me how much she admires Lady Antonia Fraser, she says she'll drive me home, she drives me home, in the car park in front of my apartment she switches off the engine, she stares at me with watery eyes, she squeezes my hand, then quickly withdraws hers, she says she has to go, she has to be home each night at 6.30pm to cook her husband dinner, it's what he expects, and now it is late December, Alicia is away someplace with her Elvis impersonator, I'm alone in the apartment, with instructions to feed the cats, for Christmas I treat myself to a copy of *The House and Garden Drinks Guide*, I read *Farewell, My Lovely*, thinking of Honey and feeling sorry for myself I listen repeatedly to 'Just Like Tom Thumb's Blues', I buy the new Neil Young album, *Zuma*, a good album to drink to, after more liquor than is good for me I spill candlewax across it which solidifies in the grooves, I buy Joni Mitchell's new album *The Hissing of Summer Lawns*, it's a crushing disappointment after her previous albums, I continue to accumulate receipts from Government Liquor store #210 at 2050 West 41st Avenue, I spend Christmas alone, I watch a lot of TV, I watch *Dr Phibes Rises Again*, I think it's terrific, I watch *Lost Horizon*, the musical, Hollywood handmaidens sing, John Gielgud leads the way with twenty-four monks to sunlit Shangri-La, Peter Finch stumbles over a ridge with an idiot's grin while a heavenly chorus sobs 'everyone has a lost horizon', and now I am through Christmas, now it's January, Alicia returns from wherever she's been, she gives me a book of Maxfield Parrish posters and a Honolulu shell plantpot, I give her a coffee table book about cats (how I've changed, Louise, exclamation mark) and a wooden music box, I bought it in Camden market, when you open the lid it plays a slow, tinkly version of 'Für Elise', Milena appears at the window of my carrell, she hands me a Polish honey cake, we go to a quiet bar for drinks, later we walk in the darkness and the rain, I want to show you the first snowdrops in Vancouver, she says softly, they grow by a boiler manhole under a tree in a garden, we walk to this place and stand there in the darkness, gazing at these white shapes, it's 9.30pm and she has to go, the next day, it's five in the afternoon, the buildings are once more blotted out by a dense sea mist, freighters hoot in English Bay like big distant animals in pain, such style, the minutes pass, the fog licks at my window on Level 8, the animals are still in pain, I have identified them, they are elephants crying mournfully as they form a group and kneel, George Orwell is shooting them one by one, see how they fall and lie down and die together in a lake of blood, that evening I went alone to see *The Mysterious Monsters*, a smash-hit documentary which had just opened at five Vancouver cinemas simultaneously, it's mostly about Bigfoot, it is claimed that these shy legendary humanoids inhabit the remote rain-forests of the Pacific Northwest, they live on berries, sometimes they disturb people in remote houses by punching in their windows when they are watching TV, no one has yet shot one, *The Mysterious Monsters* is narrated by 'The Man From Glad', he is like Mr Clean, he is another deodorised hunk of hairy masculinity who pops up regularly on TV, he fractures every

TV movie, his role is to interrupt the action with other action, he is is shown punching a garbage bag but no matter how much he batters the bag he can't hurt it, he confides: *Glad garbage bags, the strong ones!* Canadian television is full of surprises, I feel like The Man Who Fell to Earth, amazed by the strangeness of the aliens of planet earth, I am especially startled when Captain James T. Kirk of the Starship *Enterprise* appears on the TV screen holding a gladioli and urging viewers to make sure to buy their vegetables from a leading chain of British Columbia supermarkets, Captain how could you sink so low? *Zuma* is a brilliant album but it says nothing to me at this point in my turning life, *The Hissing of Summer Lawns* was a waste of five dollars, jazz and bongo drums are not my thing, not then and not now, sorry, years later I read that the *Zuma* song 'Stupid Girl' is supposed to be about Joni Mitchell and that her song 'The Circle Game' is a response to Young's 'Sugar Mountain' and now it is the second day of January of the new year and it's snowing on West 41st Street, there's something I've been meaning to tell you, Milena says when I next go for coffee with her, she tells me that if I want to understand her marriage I should read 'How I Met My Husband' by Alice Munro, I quickly get hold of a copy, I sit down and read it in one go, it's a terrible story, I don't mean that in a lit crit sense, I mean in what this story reveals about love and deception, what it tells me about Milena and her marriage to Waclaw Slabczynski, Waclaw pronounced *vazz-laff*, who is, obviously, Polish, 'How I Met My Husband' is about a naïve and innocent girl in Canada who falls in love with an aviator, he's only passing through, he flirts with the girl, they embrace and cuddle, he could easily seduce her but he holds off, he promises that they'll meet again, he says he'll write her a letter, he'll tell her where he is and she can come see him, he departs, after that she goes out to wait by the mailbox every day, day after day after day, but no letter ever comes, in the end she realises that the aviator is never going to write, this knowledge makes her heart heavy as a lump of lead, she stops waiting by the mailbox, then the mailman telephones, he tells her he misses her, they date, they marry, they procreate, the mailman likes to tell the children how their mother hooked him by waiting for him to come to the mailbox every day, *I laugh and let him because I like for people to think what pleases them and makes them happy*, it's a story about a romantic dream which vanishes like morning mist, it's about recognising that true love will never happen in your life so you may as well settle for marriage to a man who is decent and good, it's about human need and human endurance, better a hollow marriage to a man you don't love than life as a spinster forever dreaming of Mr Right, a little later M tells me she and Waclaw don't have sex any more, but that's what adulterers always tell those they have sex with, and if you can deceive your spouse, you can surely deceive your lover too, I was always waiting for something in this life she says, her eyes brimming, fixed on mine, back at the apartment Alicia tells me she has cancer, Oh, I say, I'm sorry to hear that, I am not sure I really believe her, it's caused by cosmic radiation, she says, air crews get it more than other people, who told you this? I ask, Tom, she says, who is Tom? Tom is a doctor, she is dating him now, evidently the pudgy Elvis imperson-ator is toast, she told Tom she had a pain in her ribs, he thinks it might be cancer, he gave her an examination, yes, I damned well bet he did, a perfect excuse Louise to fondle a woman's breasts, Milena says she'll give me another ride home, it's a little out of her way, we go to West 41st by way of Marine Drive, Alicia isn't there, I invite Milena in to meet the cats, she likes cats, she makes a fuss of them, they raise their tails and stare at her with disdain, these are super-cool cats, this evening the archives indicate I drank two ouzos, three gin-and-tonics, a whiskey sour and seven bottles of Toby, Milena blows me a kiss as she leaves, outside it is raining, I wonder what her husband will think of her getting in at one in the morning, and now it is mid-January, Milena takes me out to dinner, she phones home to say pressure of work is detaining her at her office, Waclaw tells her to come home at once, she says she won't and puts the phone down, she drives me home, she's a little tipsy, she says she's not playing games with me, her perfume wafts over me, lilac and something musky, many years later I read *Perfume*, it was better than I expected, her lips are greedy for mine, this cannot end here, I am his wife, she says, a flake of dialogue that howls for an accompanying shrug, and then she adds, anticipating Prince Charles, *whatever that means*, Waclaw, plump, selfish, complacent, why had she married him? why did a woman of fire attach herself to such a dried-up pedant? it's *Middlemarch* all over again, Course and Professor Evaluation Published by the Arts Undergraduate Society, Political Science 300 – Professor W. C. Slabczynski, Political Science 300 is a survey of political thought from Plato to the nineteenth century, students by and large felt that the material was worthwhile and necessary, but there was much criticism of the organization and presentation of the course, Prof. Slabczynski was sharply criticised for his monotonous rendition of his 'yellowed lecture notes' and for his apparent unwillingness to face questions in class, students felt that his approach to the course stifled any interest and enthusiasm, and several suggested that the lectures simply be mimeographed instead, students complained of 'the total lack of feedback' and some made facetious and coarse suggestions which cannot be reproduced here, marking was fair but slightly low, some felt that the historical approach produced an emphasis on 'memorizing' and that the structure of the course left no time for critical analysis of the material, I look him up, he's the author of *The Myth of Democracy* and *The Menace of Liberalism*, they have copies in the library, he's distinguished, black rounded letters attach themselves barnacle-like to the rump of his name, honorificabilitudinitatibus is truly the word, I hurry off to the dark bowels of the stacks where I'll find 'Political Science', the lighting in the basement stacks is poor, the slender fluorescent strips on the high ceiling are disfigured by dark internal growths, like an X-ray showing multiple tumours, I also have to meet the challenge of the Dewey Decimal System and its interminable fractions and sub-fractions, at one point a cobweb attaches itself to my hair and another one to my arm, in the end, draped in torn spider traps, I locate The Husband's two books, by the time I've found them I feel like Miss Havisham, awash in spiders' webs and dust-laden decay, an apt analogy in some respects, for the wedding cake is surely stale and dappled with mildew, opening his books I see that the first one was last taken out four years earlier, and the other one has never been borrowed, it even has uncut pages, I take them upstairs to be stamped by Greensleeves and go back on the bus with them to West 41st Avenue, there I quickly discover (the titles are a clue) that W. C. Slabczynski is somewhere to the Right of Genghis Khan, he doesn't like democracy, he deplores it, he likes *authority*, which should always reside in *a sovereign body*, he loathes *popular sovereignty* which is the expression of *the secret, irrational urges of the common man*, in Professor Slabczynski's ideal society government would be in the hands of *a sovereign body* comprised of *the most educated and intelligent people*, he emphasises that it is especially important to include Political Scientists in this sovereign body, as they are more intelligent and objective than The Common Man, Professors from the most respected universities should also be enrolled in this supreme organ of governance, this is because

Professors are men of experience and great learning, their convictions are based on *objective knowledge*, the problem with so-called democracy as it currently exists is that *opinion* has supplanted *objective knowledge*, this new sovereign body will require leadership, Group Leadership never works and therefore a single individual should take on this role, it is unfortunate that *Führer* – 'leader' – is a word and a concept which has fallen into a certain disrepute because of the actions of one historical individual who, though in many ways a visionary and an idealist, regrettably failed to live-up to acceptable standards, one makes no excuses, one clear conclusion which might be drawn from this and other recent historical trends is that governance of any modern society would be best placed in the hands of a Professor of Political Science, a man of established authority whose sound judgement was not in doubt, I gulp down a bottle of sweet white wine and move on to *The Menace of Liberalism*, a word which to me means creepy Jeremy Thorpe, a dead dog, the nude figure of Norman Scott flaunting his buttocks on the cover of *Private Eye*, Liberalism I learn from Professor Slabczynski is the ideology which saps the Free World, it makes a fetish of voting and election by majority participation, ignoring the reality that this half-educated majority lacks any rational recognition of what best represents its own interests, it values pluralism, which implicitly acknowledges that the average man is mentally weak and uninformed and lacks a proper understanding of good taste and civic responsibility, Liberalism seeks to legitimise itself by means of elections, substituting populism for superior and more desirable choices, this simply opens the gates to those who would subvert society, and so it went on, page after page after page, it was like an editorial in a tabloid newspaper, reprocessed as grey academic prose: criminals were pampered! judges had their hands tied!

abolitionists sought to protect murderers by campaigning against the death penalty! more bombs should be dropped on Vietnam! no wonder he was not popular with his students, Professor Slabczynski was a fascist pig, but this tosh made him popular in certain places, he has regular invitations to South Africa, there are American colleges which invite him to address the faculty on the internal threats faced by the Free World, and Milena wants me to meet him, face to face, she says, as I stickily lie on top of her in a post-coital haze of rosy well-being, face to face, eh? I remark dryly, repeating her words, she looks puzzled, then understands, beast! she squeals, and I harden inside her and it begins again, yes Louise, we finally fucked, she drove me to my apartment one afternoon when Alicia was in the air and we stripped off and climbed on to my single bed, she startled me by dropping down to my crotch, she was a gobbler, I pushed her away, I did not want that, but I am not liberated woman she protested, in that unusual sing-song accent of hers where middle Europe swims with North America, I take no pills, no problem dearest, L, always alert to wondrous possibility, happens to be in possession of a packet of contraceptives, L lets her force the rubber down around his granite shaft etcetera and it begins, continues until she calls out words L doesn't understand, after which L lets himself go, matching her spasms with his own, they are lovers, and now it is the start of February, according to *The Vancouver Sun* it's the third day of the New Year in the Chinese lunar calendar, a newspaper which the manuscripts reveal Malcolm Lowry liked to call *The Hangover Moon*, now it's the Year of the Dragon and goodbye to the Year of the Rabbit, *Dragon's years are believed to be times of dramatic, constructive change*, yeah, right, another ice-cold sea fog drifts in and envelops my world, the rabbit-hole is magical, twenty minutes later the fog fades and retreats across the steaming waters of the estuary, I start reading Henry Troyat's biography of Gogol, I learn that from an early age Gogol tried to *preserve a zone of darkness around himself*, I spent three dollars fifty on going to see *Hustle*, mainly because it had Catherine Deneuve in it, it was memorable only for the line, *Every man has his white whale, and when he finds it it destroys him*, most evenings Milena has to be with her husband, she can't come to see movies with me, so I go alone, I go to see *Candy*, with Richard Burton terrific as the Canadian poet Irving Layton, but apart from that... just a sequence of monotonous copulation fantasies yet no female nudity at all Louise, and so the days pass, Vancouver has a tramp, I spot him often in the streets between downtown and UBC and West 41st, maybe it's because I walk a lot and ride buses a lot, I'm alert to the street action, the tramp looks like Karl Marx, he wears a plastic raincoat and carries a tent and a rucksack, I saw him the other day, sat on a bench near the park on Arbutus, I noticed he was reading *The New York Review of Books*, perhaps, I think, bleakly-mournfully, perhaps this is me in thirty years' time... Laurence Sterne's ninth letter to Eliza: *You owe much, I allow, to your husband, you owe something to appearances, and the opinion of the world; but, trust me, my dear, you owe much likewise to yourself*, my Larkin phase continues, now I am reading *The North Ship*, I write to my Scandinavian friend in London, Jan Janssen, I tell him 'Nursery Tale' sums it all up, a weariness of daybreak, spread with carrion kisses, carrion farewells, Milena takes me to see *The Queen of Spades*, she is fanatical about opera, we sit in the expensive fourteen-dollar seats, at the front, in this opera the hero becomes entangled with a woman who throws herself off a cliff, later he shoots himself, the internet is not yet invented, the *Vancouver Sun* keeps me in touch with world events, I learn that the Vatican has issued a declaration on sexual ethics, re-stating the

54

Catholic Church's position against the sins of sex outside marriage, homosexuality and masturbation, later in the paper I read how Milo Haughman, a leading American furniture designer, is spearheading the move to use books as part of the décor of the home, yes, books are finally IN as decorating devices, books fill rooms with warmth, mellowness, meaning and character, I read that the American designer Angelo Donghia is in the habit of leaving books open and lying casually here and there, as if he has just been momentarily interrupted from reading, on the news-stands of this city I notice (pay attention, Louise) there's a glossy magazine called *Pacific Affairs*, notions of freedom are tied up with drink, Malcolm Lowry wrote that, Milena takes me to see the film of *The Joke*, it's every bit as good as the book, a hero torn between Marketa, a woman he loves but who rejects him, and Helen, who he is indifferent to but who desires him, along the way there's a suicide, a failed suicide, and a lot of shots of the protagonist walking alone down deserted streets, next day Milena gives me a copy of *The Rubaiyat of Omar Khayyam* and a red rose, she has underlined parts, I buy another Joni Mitchell LP, *Ladies of the Canyon*, my favourite track is the last song on the first side, 'The Arrangement' is a bitter song about a lover who is married and who won't let go of the marriage or the material comforts of an agreeable bourgeois lifestyle, the sadness and anger Mitchell puts into the last articulation of the word 'more' in the repeated refrain *you could have been more* still haunts me all these decades later, and so the days go by, the local radio keeps playing 'Hurricane' and 'Fifty Ways to Leave Your Lover', Milena still wants me to meet her husband, we have been fucking for several weeks and now *she really really wants me to meet her husband*, weird, it makes me kinda nervous, I really don't understand The Psychology of Woman, I still don't Louise, he doesn't have a clue what's going on, in fact, Milena says, he's commented how much happier she's seemed recently – but all the same... this guy is an extreme reactionary, if he finds out I'm his wife's lover he might shoot me! after all, in the war, she told me, he served in the Polish army, I know nothing about weaponry but this guy does, or he might just snatch up a kitchen knife and plunge it into my heart, a crime of passion, a jealous husband outraged that the sacred institution of marriage has been defiled, his defence barrister would sleekly argue that it was a moment of madness, the florid judge would ooze sympathy for the defendant – a plump white man in his fifties, with right-wing views just like his own – the deceased was a young man whose hair, frankly, was far too long, probably a druggie, Not Guilty! *oh don't be a goody-cooper!* cries Milena, when I unfold my anxieties, her bright eyes are full of merriment, a *giddy-kipper*, I say, correcting her lamentable pronunciation, she tells me not to be so silly, Waclaw never cooks, he simply wouldn't know which drawer holds the kitchen knives, and he hasn't fired a gun since the war, and that was a rifle, besides he doesn't own any guns, relax, she wins me round, gobble, gobble, yes, how can I deny her anything? outside intercourse she is mad about two things, the first is opera, the second is skiing, we've done *The Queen of Spades* and *The Seagull*, now it's time for the other thing, she rolls up at 6.30am on a Sunday to take me up to the mountains for the day, but I am from the arid English flatlands, I have never skied in my life, snow is a rare substance, we go to a centre where she rents me a pair of skis, I strap them on, she tells me I have good poise and balance, we ski six miles down a mountainside, an easy slope, I'm relieved when I make it down without falling or breaking bones, we return my rented skis and go to the bar for a beer and some conversation, then on to a restaurant, later we return to her car, there's a pamphlet tucked under the wipers, *Confess that you are a guilty sinner in God's sight, for you have broken his commandments*, it says, yes, really, and we move off along the long winding road back to Vancouver, from the radio Canned Heat sing 'On The Road Again', then Melanie comes on, celebrating her brand new pair of roller skates, then Milena switches off the music and I take out my copy of *Old Possum's Book of Practical Cats* and recite the entire collection to her, while she breaks into peals of laughter and shrieks with delight (this is sounding like *Un homme et une femme*, n'est-ce pas Louise?) and in the next scene we are at a wine and cheese party, at the Slabczynski apartment, a select gathering of some twenty people from the university, colleagues, Orla the Irish head of Special Collections, et moi, the youngest, Milena leads me over to him, this is L, she explains, I have mentioned him, he is researching the manuscripts of Malcolm Lowry, Malcolm Lowry? his eyes tighten, Professor Slabczynski scowls, he has dimly heard of Malcolm Lowry, a disreputable drunk, one of those Romantic self-destructive types, deplorably weak, a self-indulgent individual who would have benefited from getting up in the morning to go to an office and do a sober hard day's work! but then good manners kick in, scholarship in no matter how degenerate a form must be respected, and I am English, he has always admired the English, without them Europe would be a different place today, Waclaw reminds me of the Buddha – plump, affable, smiling, plus bald on top, he has a third chin growing under the big second one, no wonder she's sexually bored by this lump, she says he hasn't fucked her for five years, the oldest of adulterer narratives, *My spouse doesn't understand me, we no longer have sex*, but if he ever does heave that vast tub of flesh on top of her and press his penis into her, it's surely all over very quickly, he doesn't consider her, it's not something I want to think about but if I do have to think about it it's as something quick and unsatisfactory, I'd imagined Waclaw as hard in other ways, a domineering and aggressive right-winger, fierce and furious in debate, loud as any bully, but on the contrary he's as timid as a dormouse, his voice is soft and low, his demeanour a little shy and ingratiating, he dreams of utopian tyrannies but seems weak and uncharismatic, we exchange pleasantries, do I like Vancouver? yes, very much, thank you, our conversation fizzles and sputters, I have no interest in Political Science and he has no interest in *Under the Volcano*, I drift off to get another beer, I stay long enough to have fulfilled my social duties, then I scarper, I can't bear to be in a room with Milena like this pretending to be just a vague acquaintance, something tears at my heart, she sees me to the door, we have to go on pretending, I'll see you in Special Collections, I mutter, Yes, I expect so, but then she follows me out into the lobby and closes the door behind her, she grabs hold of me, recklessly presses her lips against mine, then pulls back, I luff you SO MUCH, she whispers, and then she's gone back into her apartment and I'm trudging down the cold concrete steps of the stairwell Louise, then night, then day, then her biography, her autobiography, she'd missed out on years of sex – both before and after marriage – she didn't lose her virginity until she was twenty-nine, it happened in New York, he was a trainee architect, Raymond, she still has his photograph, black and white, three by three, a grinning row of perfect teeth, the hair brushed back, the swaggering pose beside a nineteen-fifties sports car, his hand resting on the elegant curve of a front mudguard just as it would lie on the breast of a woman he'd just penetrated, Raymond, smartly dressed practised predator, Raymond, charming Brylcreem'd seducer of beautiful inexperienced women, it didn't last, of course, Raymond's wandering eye soon wandered on to fresh cleavage, a year later she married Waclaw, now she's the one in control, another furtive car trip, she turns off the engine, she stares at me with watery eyes, she takes my hand, she caresses my face, she quotes from a Czech novelist, Ivan Klíma, who wrote: *In a deaf and blinded world a kindred soul can be found*, Oh, L she whispers, her eyes fix on me with extreme desire, I think I made you up inside my head, she said, and then you appeared and it turned out you really existed, ARTS CALENDAR English 360 – Dr Militká Slabczynski, This course deals with Sixteenth and early Seventeenth-Century drama, authors studied are Marlowe, Shakespeare, Middleton, Jonson, Webster and Ford, a great deal of criticism and analysis is allowed, discussion ranges widely and is not restricted to drama only, the workload was found to be reasonable, the class was large, Dr Slabczynski was found to be extremely knowledgeable, fair, and willing to listen and even learn (oh rarity) from her students, she was able to pass on her own enthusiasm for the subject to her students and was rated as superlative all round, an asset to the Department and a must for those who take their English literature seriously, the strains of a polonaise linger in the air, a child howls, a dog barks, a sparrow lands on a rock and an avalanche begins, a miner coughs and the workings collapse all around him, I am tired of history, your father said, I have a dream of Canada, their plane touched down in the month and year when – the text snaps, Milena stares at the grey landing strip, the grey terminal building, so this is England – and somewhere out there, beyond the mists, below the stars, the patterns put upon them by puny earthlings, I am there, I am here, I am drinking too much, I am definitely drinking too much, dear Louise let me acquaint you with Alexander Pope's squib 'On a Lady Who P*ssed at the Opera', which notes that 'while others weep with emotion, She shows her grief in a sincerer place', a moist tale this also, a Sunday morning, I set my alarm so that I could be on West 10th Avenue, very early, Milena comes along in her car, she calls it 'Moritz', I jump in, she drives me up into the mountains for a day's snow-trekking, everything's fine until the drive back, when she starts crying, she tells me how old she is, L is currently twenty-seven, and she is – the road rushes at us – forty-nine, I'm... shocked, I thought she was younger, quite a bit younger, although there were always those grey hairs, forty-nine seems like someone who is well on their way to being, well, incredibly old, Shakespeare dead at fifty-two, Burbage at fifty-one, the road rushes at us, it doesn't matter, the conversation continues, I make Milena laugh, and soon everything's tickety-boo again, I utter it, all tickety-boo, she shrieks, say that again, her enthusiasm brims, this is what love does, it makes all the world sparkle, stop that, there's a word for that, sententious, what? I reply, that boo-thing, she giggles, that thing-boo! oh, you mean tickety-boo, she hoots with laughter, a good solid English phrase, I say, a little stiffly, so don't be a giddy-kipper, please, she collapses, gurgling, no of course she doesn't, she's driving a car, we arrive between the sheets, her face wrenches in a paroxysm of pleasure etcetera, she twists and presses her face deep into the pillow to muffle her loud cries, why is L reminded of Graham Greene, perhaps he only wrote one important book, one important book is all you need, one novel that stays shining in a sky dense with the Milky Way, where every day brings fresh luminosity, *The Bookseller* offers some 2021 examples: *Set in the 1970s its central character is a young boy called K who tries to navigate his way around the various prejudices and cruelties placed in his way, a story told with palpable joy in language it is also evocatively multi-layered, shot through with subtle complexity as the author flits in and out of the lives of its characters across geography and time, this is a dazzling debut novel that brilliantly explores the interconnections between race and class, it shows us that cruelty is as corrosive to the souls of its perpetrators as to its victims,* this sort of thing, such showings, such shinings, week after week these novels arrive like blazing meteorites, dropping down on to the tables in Waterstones, another is about *a man pulled back by an undying love, in 1976 Tomás Orilla is a medical student in Buenos Aires where he has moved in hopes of reuniting with Isabel a childhood crush but the reckless passion that has long drawn him is leading Isabel ever deeper into the ranks of the insurgency fighting an increasingly oppressive regime and Tomás has always been willing to follow her anywhere, to do anything to prove himself yet what exactly is he proving and at what cost to them both? it will be years before a summons back arrives for Tomás, now living as Thomas Shore in New York, it isn't a homecoming that awaits him, however, so much as an odyssey into the past, an encounter with the ghosts that lurk there, and a reckoning with the fatal gap between who he has become and who he once aspired to be, this novel has already garnered rave reviews from the likes of authors including Kamila Shamsie and Colm Tóibín, it deserves every inch of the glowing praise received, it features the most exquisite writing and mesmerising voice, it is hypnotic, it grapples with love, betrayal and guilt, it transports us to a stunningly evoked Buenos Aires,* meanwhile, over in Vancouver, Milena is full of sweet little surprises, once, after a fuck, she leaned over me and recited a few lines of Shakespeare, I knew she knew Shakespeare but I didn't know she knew any Shakespeare off by heart, My bounty is as boundless as the sea my love as deep the more I give to thee the more I have, for both are infinite, she is – this is the word – intense, more intense than any woman I have ever known, her passion for me is spectacular, your eyes, she says, they are so wonderful, words articulated in that unique cracked stretched accent, I hear her voice even now, it jostles with the

61

other voices, it is as distinct as Honey's, or as yours Louise, Milena's eyes are green, marble green, a couple of women before Milena have complimented me on my eyes, but no one has ever said to me what she says next: Yours eyes are like cornflower-blue sapphires with lights behind them, has she been reading the letters of Héloïse and Abelard? I wonder, I remember that her favourite cultural form is opera, looking back, I find it hard to remember the individual acts of lovemaking, they blur, when we could, husband permitting, we fucked once or twice a day, sometimes three times, on one occasion four times, and now it is Valentine's Day, we meet for coffee at, hey, Mozart Coffee, this is on Robsonstrasse, Milena gives me an LP, *The Magic Flute*, I give her a children's book about – forgive me, Louise – a lonely little caterpillar which suddenly turns into a gorgeous butterfly, plus a bunch of yellow tulips, plus a heart on a stick, next Milena drives me to the airport, a place where we can safely be alone together, she is constantly nervous someone will see us, we go there to sit in the plush bar, I stare out at the long shimmering runways and the sunlight stabbing down over stormy Vancouver Island, we talk of Plath, of Trakl, of Keats, of matters of the heart, she has to go East – a conference – and the plan is for me to go too, February 29, the first of five nights at the Château Laurier, Ottawa, the city is deep in snow, we meet up, embrace, tear off our clothes and spring into bed, later we have caviar sent up on room service, plus a roast dinner, plus wine, she has an American Express card, in Ottawa, Louise, we went to see *Jaws*, *The Romantic Englishwoman*, *One Flew Over the Cuckoo's Nest* and *The Man Who Would Be King*, I return via Toronto, a sub-plot which need not concern you, sometimes there are backstories which have no narrative function, they are merely life, which is too complex for literary fiction, this backstory is surplus to requirements, at Toronto Airport they are asking for Mr Kafka to please go to the Air Canada supervisor's desk immediately, yes, really, truly, life is so much better than literary fiction, on the way there the taxi drove past a large sign that read HELP CRIPPLED CIVILIANS, and now we are back on the west coast, in the last week of March we go to the City Nights cinema at 150 E. Hastings to see the 7.30pm performance of *Don't Look Now*, I've seen it before and I want her to see it, I think at twenty-seven it's one of the best movies ever made, I still think that, one day I thought I'll go to Venice and check out all those places where Donald Sutherland and Julie Christie walk and run and shout, a promise to myself I later kept, though it took me many years to get there, and I was not with Milena but someone else, as we enter the cinema I realise that the music which is being played in the lobby is Joni Mitchell's best album, *Blue*, these fragments drawn from old notebooks, letters and a diary I have shored against my ruins, there is something about T. S. Eliot, is there not? even P. J. Harvey and Lana Del Rey have paid homage, we slept together at the Thunderbird Motor Inn, 1225 N. Wenatchee Avenue, Washington 98801, Oral Roberts (*sic*) was on TV, evangelising, the programme cut to bachelor boy Cliff Richard, our fresh-faced Christian was in occupied Galilee, under a blue sky, rowing a boat, Milena said: I need to go pee-pee, she went to the john, she closed the door, Hey! I shout, why are you closing the door? I open it, I say: We are lovers, you do not need to hide away like this, how her eyes flash! no man has ever seen me urinate! she says, there's a first time for everything, I retort, I hold back the door, she smilingly capitulates, she hoists her skirt and drops her knickers and squats, she smiles shyly, she starts to piss, the jet of urine hisses and splashes in the bowl, she dabs herself dry with a tissue, I stare entranced at her black bush, haven't you read James Joyce? I ask, of course she bloody has, it's just that she's not all that keen on his writing, many years later Louise I saw the Antonioni film *Identificazione di una donna* and I was reminded, oh yes I was reminded, I am now this month at this time reading Chekhov, who wrote: People are having a meal, just having a meal, but at the same time their happiness is being created or their lives are being smashed up, I am reading on Milena's recommendation *The Seagull*, it's a play about a woman in love with a man in love with a woman who has casual sex with a predatory hack writer, who dumps her, the hero, if such he is, would like to be a writer but in the end throws his manuscript into the stove, at the end the main characters are playing cards when the hero shoots himself off-stage, Milena drives me to Seattle for two days and two sweet nights, to see some opera, her husband doesn't like opera, gullible Waclaw thinks she's gone alone, at the border a man in uniform writes down my name and UK address, when he is done he says: Have a good time, Ellis, I nod, thanks, I hope to, how nice and friendly they are at the American border, we stay at The Bridge Motel, 3650 Bridge Way North (38th and Aurora), gone now, it's a Saturday, she's brought me here for sex and to take me to the Seattle Opera House to see Thomas Pasatieri's *The Seagull*, the libretto expands the role of Masha and adds an aria by Madame Arkadina, who sings of her great success on stage as Queen Jocasta, I have no memory of this opera at all, it washed over me and drained away into oblivion, next day it rains, we go to a movie theater to see Bergman's *The Magic Flute*, this is altogether more memorable, we eat at the Holiday Inn, the serving napkin has a full-colour reproduction of the Declaration of Independence, back over the border she phones her husband, *Get back as soon as you can*, he says, *I need my supper*, returning to Vancouver I discover that Alicia wants me out, in two weeks and five days she is marrying her doctor, Tom, he calls round and we meet, he is tanned, with a rectangular face, very short hair, perfect fangs, and a deeply insincere smile, his manner is that of a used-car salesman, a crust of charm over the hard-sell, he wasn't really a doctor, I no longer remember every detail, perhaps he played rugby, he was certainly sporty, it's really great to meet you, L, You too, Tom, whatever he was called, Alicia is away on my last evening, Milena visits, we fuck, I move out next day, Alicia turns up to collect my key, I wish her well and say I hope she'll be very happy with her hunk (they do seem matched), she says she hopes I'll call round for a drink before I depart for England, I say I will, but she never gets in touch again and I wouldn't have bothered anyway, I find a basement room at 3768 W.18th Avenue, it is let by a Swede who lives above, in the main house, he's converted his basement into two rooms, separated by panelling, a silent Chinese man lives in the other room, I nod at him and he nods back, we hold no conversation, we are partners only in sharing a life beneath the floorboards of a middle-class home, like mice, I suppose Kafka comes to mind, also that Russian, my room is dark and, yes yes yes my paperbacks whisper a thin adjective: *Dostoievskyan*, there is one tiny window through which I can see thistles pressing against the glass and the wall of the house next door, but – plus point – I am only two hundred yards from a liquor store, I am reading the Canadian poet, Patrick Lane, his poem 'At the Edge of the Jungle' really hits the spot, *I am grown older than I imagined: the garden I dreamed does not exist and compassion is only the beginning of suffering, Everything deceives*, Milena calls by in the afternoons and we fuck to the soundtrack of a Bach cantata, and now it is All Fools' Day, I am back at Vancouver Airport to say goodbye to Milena, she is jetting off to Edmonton, for a conference of the editorial committee of *The Canadian Journal of Comparative Literature*, the next day I am back at the airport to welcome her home, she races over to the barrier and hisses that I mustn't kiss her because there's someone from UBC on the plane who knows her, L is a Taurean, L looks at his horoscope in the *Province* (that's Vancouver's morning paper, Louise), *Make sure you please higher-ups today since they can help you advance more quickly, be an excellent citizen, and gain benefits, this evening will be ideal for entertaining,* what I claim is to live to the full the contradiction of my time, which may well make sarcasm the condition of truth, Roland Barthes wrote that, and now it is the first Saturday in the April of that year, the sirens wail downtown, in doorways beetroot-faced alcoholics twangle strange instruments and cry out for small change, on Granville short-skirted lipsticked teenage girls openly exchange joints, emotional traffic cops scream at transgressive pedestrians, at the Eve cinema they are showing *The Sinful Bed* and *The Sinful Dwarf*, I pay a visit to the socialist bookshop on skid row, a tiresome little boy runs around with a red balloon, smacking it against the customers, including me, while his mother, a faded hippy in a long floral dress, tells him to stop it, Otherwise it will burst, she says, adding: like capitalism, yes, she really did say that, I buy *The Feminine Mystique* and *Modern Women in Love*, hoping, Louise, to enlarge my very restricted understanding of this – ouch! – mysterious species, and now Milena threatens to kill herself, she says she can't bear to be torn between her husband and L, then leave him, I say, I can't she replies, I'd rather die, I don't take her seriously, I hug her, kiss her, tell her I love her, Milena tells me of people she has known who have killed themselves, they include one of her supervisors at Toronto, plus the Dean of the Arts Faculty, several years ago, the last Saturday in March of that year, I am in Seattle again with Milena, we are there to see *Aida* at the Opera House, does she like opera because her life is operatic? a stray thought, as entertainment goes it's okay, *Aida* is about a man in love with a slave girl from Ethiopia, her father looks like Jimi Hendrix, he is busy invading Egypt, the hero, in turn, is loved by the king's daughter, a sensual 200-pound beauty, some of the performances strike me as wooden, the hero lacks charisma, there is a chorus of men in Roman tunics with bare skinny legs and knobbly knees, and the scenery belongs to the world of amateur dramatics, but hey, what do I know about opera? after sex that night Milena tells me her period is three and a half weeks overdue, it's now late April, summer's here, the skies are blue, day after day, seagulls cruise overhead in gangs, riding the thermals, screeching, on the grassy spaces of the campus people sit around, chatting, smiling, happy, re-reading *The Selected Letters of Malcolm Lowry* I discover that in the summer of 1951 the writer sketched out the plot of a novel he never wrote, its chief character, he explained, was troubled by many things, *A stormy love affair with an older woman, a Dostoievskian brother, the ghoulishness of his contemporaries, the ideology of the English faculty, the feeling of hopelessness that overwhelms him about his choice of vocation...* Special Collections is in the news, well, in the *Vancouver Sun*, anyway, a librarianship student working in the archives has turned up a letter written in 1894 by the wife of Thomas Hardy to the mother of Lionel Haweis, she explained that Hardy's interest in the cause of women's suffrage is, in a word, nil, *He understands only the women he invents – the others not at all*, considering the number of essays and theses that have been written on Thomas Hardy's understanding of women, *this letter is an amazing discovery*, my life has turned into an Iris Murdoch novel, I spend the afternoon in bed with Milena and then visit her apartment that evening for two hours of conversation with her husband, we drink gin and tonics, he is amiable and unsuspecting, the next day he accuses her of being too long taking the car to the car wash, he doesn't realise I'm there too, while the huge rollers rub backwards and forwards against the side windows, drowning them in foam, we embrace, we are still kissing when the process finishes in jets of cold water, I am drunk not only with love, I am holding a bottle of beer and I spill it on the carpeted floor, No! she cries, in horror, Waclaw will smell it! let him, I laugh, No, no! I press my lips to her mouth, she moans and grips me tightly, the attendant gives us a suspicious stare, his mouth tightens with disapproval, this ain't right, next day we have a narrow escape, she picks me up on the campus and drives me to W.18th Avenue, we stop off on the way at 4501 West 10th Avenue so that I can get some cash out of my local branch of the Royal Bank of Canada, while I am inside the bank Waclaw strolls past, he has gone out to do some shopping, he is amazed to see his wife sitting alone in the car, parked right there on West 10th, he walks over and asks her what on earth she's doing there when she said she had a tutorial on campus at this time, in a panic she says she's on her way to get the winter tires changed over at the garage, astutely the mad professor notices that the car has already had its winter tires switched back to the summer ones, she claps her hand to her brow, a grand operatic gesture, I am such a fool! she says, and then I rock up with my dollars, I don't spot Waclaw until it's too late, L! she shrieks, you too! how the coincidences are piling up! this is a useful liquid, it oils many plots, truly there is a stronger hand than chance which writes our affairs, she manages a tight desperate deceiving grin for Waclaw, you see, she says, it seems half the world is on this street this afternoon! I am going to the campus, L, she says, can I give you a ride? thank you, that would be most helpful, I will see you later, she says to Waclaw, he scowls as we drive away, she performs some complicated manoeuvres to create the illusion that we are heading back west, when we are really going south and then east, it seems he still doesn't suspect, though, but then in that pre-internet age only a diseased mind could imagine that a 49-year-old married woman is involved with a lover some twenty-two-years younger than her, she tells me that her husband refers to me as 'That boy', in an avuncular, paternalistic way, and now it's the merry, merry month of May, summer term and the academic year end, the students go home, or to vacation jobs, or abroad on holiday, the great library closes early, Vancouver is now very hot, Waclaw jets off to England, he has research to do at a library in London, then he's off to apartheid South Africa, where the white universities like his style of political philosophy, she writes to him, as a good wife should, regular letters, no mobile phones then, adultery was easier then, she doesn't mention I've moved into the apartment, I discover they have separate beds, I sleep in Milena's bed and she sleeps in Waclaw's bed, I'm nervous about the arrangement, this is a familiar narrative device, I've seen this situation in so many movies and TV dramas, the spouse returns to find his or her adulterous Other engaged in loud coitus, maybe that's why she writes to him so often, to check everything is going fine for him, but he never replies, he's a monster of egocentricity and self-regard, and substantially overweight too, that belly, why did she ever chain herself to this fat oaf? Orla once said the same, the woman who is in charge of Special Collections, she knew them both, Milena so full of zest for life, with a husband who was a dull lump, a mystery, Milena gets a telegram from Durban, he tells her to send one of his books by airmail, IMMEDIATELY, WITHOUT ANY DELAY, it's called *Understanding U.S. Foreign Policy*, he had it privately printed, I'm not surprised, I read it while she's out, it's a bland defence of U.S. policy, with a particular focus on Vietnam, he argues that the U.S. should be using more weapons against the Viet Cong, there is too much

American concern for human life, he argues, utterly without irony, civilian casualties are regrettable, he writes, but a victory for Communism would be far worse, for if South Vietnam falls then Communism will spread, taking over Cambodia, Malaya, Burma, quite possibly India, he's nuts, I buy the new Stones album, *Black and Blue*, we go to the States for a weekend of skiing on Mount Baker, back in Vancouver we go to see *Robin and Marian* which mingles blood-and-guts realism with sentimentality and becomes at times Monty Pythonesque: *Jump! But I might hurt myself*, Milena recommends a Czech poet called Vladimir Holan, I check him out, one line springs out at me, *I see an avalanche coming*, her taste in literature is better than her taste in popular music or husbands, she likes, oh dear, the Tijuana Brass, especially their version of 'A Taste of Honey', my time with the manuscripts was over, I'd learned all I could, I'd spent months wandering the labyrinth of the Gabriola manuscripts, I was befogged by tiny details, I was uncertain if Lowry chose this island for the sake of a pun (for its name surely invokes that of his lost tormenting faithless love Jan Gabrial), Jan who'd slipped from view, who in 1973 evaded Lowry's first biographer Douglas Day who wrote: *One would like to wish her well, but she has disappeared*, a vanishing trick accomplished primarily because her name was fake and academics were easily befogged, though truth to tell Day was far brighter than the dullard fuddled Cambridge night school professor Muriel who I met when she dropped by at Special Collections and who to my amazement was laboriously copying by hand a typed short-story she could have photocopied in two minutes flat, the arid dimwit who wrote in her inept forgotten book that Jan was a stunt girl from Hollywood films, obviously muddling her up with Margie, Muriel whose student Sean D'eath had become a friend of mine and who'd argued with her about the date of a manuscript which he'd handled and which she'd never seen, *She might contrive to look like a sweet old lady* wrote Sean *but she really is an obstinate proud old cat with a head full of 'ideas' like ½p pieces, if you meet her don't mention my name*, no, Jan was never Gabrial, for as that bloody monstrous century tottered to its end it emerged that Janine Vanderheim of Bayside, Long Island, born 11 June 1911, had adopted the pseudonym 'Jan Gabrial' initially as an actress then later as a writer, she married Lowry on 6 January 1934 when she was twenty-three, she left in '37 and filed for divorce in '39, after leaving Lowry she remarried and became Janine Singer the obscure wife of a real estate broker, at one point years later back in California she and Lowry's widow Margerie were living just ten miles from each other, they might unwittingly have passed each other in a supermarket aisle, Janine died in September 2001, at 89 she was interviewed by Stephen Lemons who wrote that she was *pixyish and fair, with lively brown eyes*, Malcolm was a very educated man she remembered, a brilliant conversationalist, he did have one problem though, a very small penis, it didn't bother me, she said, I felt we could work around it, Lowry read her diary, there she had brutally accurately described his unimpressive appendage, one time he came to the bed-side late and said Dormez, le diable est mort, though wide-awake she kept her eyes closed, it could get a little hairy she confided, I don't believe Malcolm would commit suicide she said, he was too much in love with the English language, he wasn't Joe Blow, he was, in a way, a lost soul, sometimes he left suicide notes for her to find, bluff blackmail a dipso's mental cruelty, she lived in old age in a modest home near the border of Los Angeles and Ventura counties, at least it's not about a writer, Lowry wrote of *October Ferry to Gabriola* in the margins of a letter to his American editor Albert Erskine, adding: like hell it's not, in the novel writing

71

Nothing was more unreal than a novel, even a realistic novel, Erskine asked if there was enough *narrative and dramatic (surface) interest*, because a reader wants to *feel rewarded* for reading a novel, Lowry replied that he had been reading *The Letter of Lord Chandos*, it is this aspect of it that has made it so hard for me to write he wrote referring to Herman Broch's Introduction, How, then, could he write at all? asked Herman Broch of Hugo von Hofmannsthal's creative crisis, How can muteness be abreacted with the aid of speech, moreover, Broch wrote, though the artist may establish a communion with reality in all its fluid and elusive state it must at last be broken off otherwise there would exist only work in progress, but when does this moment of completion arrive, how is this moment recognised? one answer is the lyric poem, Broch argued, since it undertook a bold irrational shortening of the chains, the change, the ch-ch-changes, in the old days it was so much easier, fourth-hand redundant adverbs were as fashionable then as today, fork off he said lovingly, you shut up she screamed floridly, but I love you he snarled harshly, how many miles to Babylon she asked reasonably, four-score-and-ten he said hopefully, that's too far she said proudly and without bitterness, is it he said extravagantly, it is she said very tenderly, it's not he said warningly, it is she said thickly, is this the end he said violently, it is she said indescribably, bayonets of ice dripped about them and a single star shone in a fountain, I have discovered a language but so complex and difficult that it would take a thousand years to synthesize a single word she added coldly, I also have discovered a language but in my language one word is the equivalent of sixteen thousand years he replied with a bitter smile, and so the years go by, I am now writing a huge and sad novel about Burrard Inlet wrote Malcolm Lowry, this was *Gabriola*, a novel that I sometimes feel could have been better stated in ten short poems – or even lines – but instead as I discovered after leaving Canada for good he does not appear to have done anything more than tinker with the primary typescript, the earliest notes for the novel were made in 1944, they were about an outbreak of fires in Ontario, its true origins lay in the journey that Lowry and wife number two made to Gabriola Island on 8 October 1946, an inconsequential trip, it inspired twenty-six pages of typescript, a story, the title the same, 'October Ferry to Gabriola', it began to swell (no innuendo, Louise) with insertions and revisions, by the end of 1953 he'd managed 206 pages, Random House dumped him, the published version which came out thirteen years after Lowry's death was compiled from 483 pages of typescript, the time-scheme is muddled, Tommy is two years old when is born, the boy due to be hanged is Chambers, then Chester, then Chapman, the paragraph order is jumbled in Chapter 22, marginalia creeps in like moss invading a patio, the author's typographical desires regarding the use of advertisements have been almost totally ignored but on the whole – cheers! – a job well done by wife number two, a text resting on a foundation of five boxes of drafts, notes, typed pages framed and pierced by marginalia, pages drowning in alternative possibilities, some 2,400 pages, in which L swam until he was exhausted, he'd seen enough, by the way did I mention that while in Vancouver I had recurring unpleasant dreams of Lowry standing at the bar of the Yew Tree in Chalvington where I once spent an afternoon drinking behind locked doors and playing left-handed table football with the landlord who obviously thought he should make some money out of the Lowry industry even if like most of the villagers he had no time for this supposed writer, Lowry was standing at the bar staring towards the rows of bottles but not at them but rather through them, as if standing on the bridge of a ship, wearing a woolly hat and looking hopelessly for land, Si, senor, that is rye whiskey, perhaps there is an advantage in withdrawing from a daily involvement in a subject while maintaining concern for it, one can think again about its basics, which become overlaid by the minutiae of scholarship, its real importance of which one need no longer so desperately reassure oneself, perhaps recapture a purely private delight in it, the joyous little lark of discursive melody soaring in some remote summer of its own above all this abyssal fury, yet furious too, with the wild controlled abandon of that music, L flew back to London, Milena will follow, L returns to Bungalow Land, L's father greeted him enthusiastically, he thrust his latest essay at his son: *THINGS ARE NOT WHAT THEY SEEM*, typed in capital letters on soft vellum, he'd made twenty copies, thank you, Smorg, I will read it, half an hour later I was sitting down at the kitchen table, the prodigal returned, before a huge oval plate of scampi and chips, afterwards I sat in one of the floral armchairs, with a mug of coffee, *Those who wish to know the moon must first look upwards, instead of spending all their lives gazing downwards at its reflection in a pool*, I read, t*hree learned men tried to understand the moon by catching it in an expensive and elaborate net but all that happened was that the moon's image became split into myriads of glittering points of light, perplexed by their failure to catch it in a net the three men strained the pool drop by drop through a series of muslin cloths of ever-finer mesh but still the moon eluded them, they went away and wrote a treatise proving that the moon has the power to shrink its bulk, transform itself into tiny particles, and then piece itself together again, in other words, a distinction must be made between Reality and its Reflection, the former lies within Man, not without, great commotion and wrong methods hinder the clear perception of Reality and Truth and lead to Wrong Ideas and a state of learned and*

74

*unlearned Ignorance*, thank you, father, most interesting, in London I rented a room for the summer, a temporary base, a fuck-pad, it was in Finchley, in a house which had been broken up into four bedsits, a shared bathroom and toilet, I had the room at the front on the ground floor, there was a boarded-up fireplace, no facilities apart from a basin with a tap and a two-bar electric fire, the fire unnecessary in the sweltering heat of that summer, also on the ground floor, at the back, with two rooms to my one, was a couple I designated as middle-aged and middle-class, perhaps bankruptcy – surely some great financial misfortune – had brought them to this parlous accommodation, I hardly ever saw them, above me, in two rooms beside the communal bathroom, were a young rowdy proletarian couple, I heard them shouting at each other from time to time, you sodding cow! you bastard! you cunt! you bastard! you bitch! you shit! their fondness for monosyllabic exchanges was striking, their dedication to anaphora was total, and also, I noticed disapprovingly, when they put their empty milk bottles out for the milkman they hadn't rinsed them as decent people did, finally there was the strange little man who lived in the attic room, and once again my paperbacks whispered *Kafka*, whispered *Dostoievsky*, he had a pointed nose, like a cartoon character, plus a deathly white complexion, his soft little face was strangely androgynous, the two couples in the house went out to work, but this strange little man must have been on state benefits, he never went anywhere, sometimes he sat on the wall outside my window, smoking, his greeting was a brief nod and a sort of squeak, he never smiled, I think he may have been a goblin, I emptied a rucksack of books and tried to focus on Malcolm Lowry until Milena arrived at Heathrow, we spent a little time in London, we met Jan Janssen at The Lamb and Flag, later we dined with him at the Venus Kebab House (corner of Percy Street, you can't miss it), it was another very warm evening, goodbye Jan Janssen, this tale moves on, before long Milena and I hired a car and headed north, we sat on the cliff above Smoo Cave and ate cheese and pickle sandwiches and stared at the foamy ocean and the soaring white angelic gulls, I spent 90p on a paperback guide to real ale pubs of Britain, going south, at The Woolpack in Keswick, I asked for a pint of John Peel's Nutty Brown Bitter, the barman gazed at me with derision, never heard of it he said, I showed him my paperback guide and pointed to the recommendation, Your book's a load of old rubbish he said with obvious satisfaction, we visited Dove Cottage and Milena photographed me standing in the sloping garden behind the house, later we cross Europe by train, we start late in the afternoon, at Calais I am very very thirsty, it is a scorching hot dry summer, all we have with us is a bottle of apricot brandy, I bought it so we could drink enough to get us some sleep on the overnight train, bad idea, I slurp its fire, I'm left thirstier than ever, and the train has no buffet car, a sign by the basin in the toilets says the water is NON-POTABLE, I hate French railways with an intensity worthy of a dehydrated Basil Fawlty, night falls, we rest against each other and doze, France is a long night of clanking machinery and obscure shouts and grey illuminated empty platforms, then dawn, colours return to the world, France fades, I close my eyes, later I open them, ZURICH the sign says, and on these lovers travel, through a hot, drowsy June morning, they sit face to face in an empty compartment, Switzerland goes past, without surprises, meadows, grass-sloped mountains, the brown dots of distant cattle, we must put our watches forward, I say, Milena looks puzzled, she's lost in an adulterer's reverie, Time, I say, we're back to English time, Middle-European time, ah, she smiles, yes, We haff left France behind, no longer French time! the wrinkles around her eyes tighten with merriment, she is going to be fifty but a ten-year-old girl sometimes emerges from that sun-beaten face, her heavy accent, emphatic at the start, rises to a sing-song at the end of every sentence, an unidentifiable accent after all those years in Canada had rubbed and rubbed at her mixed heritage of Czech and German, what time do you make it? seven ten? seven twelve! we adjust our watches to eleven minutes after, what were you thinking? I ask, just now, Nothing, she's lying, she must be, she continues: We reach Austria ver' soon, thirty-five, you'd have guessed, looking at that face, only when you drew kissing-close did you see the number of silver strands in the brushed-back black hair that spread itself wildly behind her shoulders, *Pardon*, it was the conductor, he entered and silently folded away the couch-ettes, dismantled the metal ladder and slotted it out of sight beneath the seat, now the mountains draw closer, toy chalets on the lower slopes spring into focus, now, every ten minutes or so, the train halts at smart, tidy little stations with neat beds of bright colourful alpine flowers, the carriage starts to get hotter and hotter as the blazing sun rises above the jagged white mountain crests, I get up and pull down the window a few inches, a chill gush of air rushes in, rustling Milena's hair, I catch more glints of silver, see that church! she's pointing but the train is pulling round a curve, a wall of stone presses abruptly against the track, casting a shadow, the church is gone, it had a little golden dome she says, churches fascinate her, she has an urge, a passion, for seeking them out, any kind, most recently dark sleepy little English parish churches with bees buzzing in graveyards where the gravestones are tilted at strange angles, she goes inside and sits and bows her head and closes her eyes and prays, I wander off, leaving her to her meditations, gazing idly at the effigies of kneeling Elizabethans with stiff stone ruffs holding up their heads and the brass plaques to soldiers fallen in forgotten imperial wars, I watch as she rises from her prayers and presses her little fingers into the old pew carvings, breathing with a delight that seems almost sexual, she takes joy in things, in everything, she wants to stroke every cat that wanders by or rubs itself against her legs, a little golden dome, and I reply perhaps made in Rome, for a moment she looks puzzled, then a smile radiates out, yes, she says, the sort not found at *home*, one of our lovers' games, tedious to others no doubt, rhyming conversation, a perfect poem, I reply, pronouncing it *pome*, you are cheating, only a little, cheat cheat cheat, she hurls herself at L, lightly pummelling his chest, L seizes her arms, they embrace, fiercely kiss, a Hollywood cliché, how monotonous this is for the reader, mercifully the door slams open, *Ihre Fahrkarten, bitte*, the lovers pull apart under the severe disapproving gaze of the ticket inspector, a grim sour-faced wretch with tight narrow eyes and a downturned mouth, he scrutinises suspiciously our tickets, then clips them with a sudden angry movement that sends two tiny discs of cardboard flying across the carriage, they bounce off the seat and fall to the floor, the inspector goes on his way, slamming the door behind him, the mountains get closer and closer, their slopes are covered in dark pine forests, the mountains become barer, bleaker, treeless, huge tongues of snow, gashes of outspread scree, darkness swallows everything: suddenly we've entered a long tunnel, we are inside the mountain, we cut through it like an assassin's bullet (a ridiculous simile, is it not, Louise?), we emerge the far side, blinking at the sunlight, pine trees press closer, closer, look! she shrieks, pointing, it's the border, Austria, a moment later the train begins to slow and clank to a halt, it moves into a siding, hissing steam, a great green wheeled dragon (oh *please*), drowsy yet watchful and alert, and now the customs men come aboard and stamp down the corridors, shouting German, once more the sliding door is wrenched back and a man in a black uniform stands over them, *Pab, bitte! yewer passpour plizz!* he barely looks at them, nods and hands them back, Milena's is plain green, mine is black, the British one is by far the best, with the golden lion and the unicorn groping their way round the giant orb like a drunken couple at a fancy-dress party, and the prancing woman, about to lose her pointed paper cap, seems to have broken free of her chains... the dragon shakes itself awake, it hisses loudly, it roars (perhaps not such a bad simile after all, eh Louise?), it emits a terrific siren-wail that howls away along the valley, it lurches onward, gathering speed, the great mountains of the Tyrol open up and give us entrance, that's where the full stop should come and the chapter end I suppose, but the past has no ending, the train moves at speed along a high ridge, more dark gatherings of pines flash past the window, we are just below the summer snow-line and the air is growing colder, between the flickering trees a road can be glimpsed, accompanying the railway but far below us, lower down the valley, the dragon, surviving deletion, strains and hoots and drags its heavy burden along this high secret track, outstripping the toy cars on the toy road far below, the cars look like colourful disciplined insects moving to and fro on insect business, how splendidly figurative all this is Louise, *enjoy*, and now remote desolate empty stony valleys come into view, then are quickly walled-up again... see those little metal platforms on the slopes, Milena says, pointing, no, yes, look, over there, and I spot it, a structure, it looks out of place in these wild empty heights, it resembles a spacecraft landed on a far moon, Milena explains, these objects are for the winter months, they are put there to disperse dangerous snow, to prevent avalanches, cannons are placed on the platforms and blast-off the overhanging drifts, if you look carefully you can see scorch marks, the same applies to this novella Louise, yes, oh yes, and now the train slows, a large sign: ARLBERG

TUNNEL, a small station comes into view, the train halts, sunlight shines down on the gravelled platform with wooden tubs containing yellow and white flowers, the station master hurries out with his little flag on a stick, a sack of mail is tossed down, this could be the Highlands of Scotland, then the wheels begin to roll again, clank, clank, clank, the train accelerates, it rushes through a sequence of short tunnels, then longer ones, the permutations of blackness and sudden sunlight on brilliant snow make my eyes dance with tiny dots, the penultimate tunnel – the longest one – runs on for what seems like miles, groups of workmen stand huddled in semi-circular niches in the tunnel wall, beside ventilation vents, water drips down the cold sooty brickwork, the train brakes and slows, now we begin the long descent to St Anton, the darkness of the final tunnel abruptly vanishes, wet sparkling silver walls rush past, and like a magician abruptly unfold a marvel, a sunlit green slope crammed with long descending rectangular gardens sprinkled with trees, above them chalets, many chalets, from one of these dainty structures two children wave from a balcony (where are these children now, Louise?), three adults motionless as statues stare from a garden as if seeing a train for the very first time, the loco is slowing all the time, it glides over a level-crossing, where people and a line of cars wait, *here-at-last, here-at-last* mutters the dragon, and now it hisses and squeals and finally stops with a jolt that shudders through every carriage, we pull down our cases from the rack, gather up our coats, and climb down the steps to the unBritish ground-level platform, we have to pick our way across the rails to the far platform, station officials shout, doors slam, a whistle blows, the train pulls out, on its way to Vienna, as it passes by I see it's accumulated a dozen extra carriages since Calais, I follow Milena to the station building, she speaks to one of the porters, who takes our cases, we can collect them later, then, not holding hands, we walk down the little cobbled road, past the Hotel-am-Post, to St Anton's main street, here we turn left, passing a terrace laid out with tables beneath the shade of poplars, white tablecloths flutter in the breeze, we go on, past sports shops with windows filled with ski equipment and racks of mountain boots, we pass small dark bars where climbing ivy frames the windows, there are flower-boxes outside and white metal tables at which men sit alone, reading newspapers, drinking coffee or beer, 10.45 says the clock attached to a gallows-like beam which protrudes from the timbered Sports Hotel, across the road is the *Reisebüro*, Milena speaks to one of the stern unsmiling young women behind the counter, a short conversation; a telephone call; a nod of the head, a room for us has been reserved, while all this is going on I gaze round at the bright blue and white posters of dazzling athletic figures spurting snow as they zig-zag down pristine mountain slopes, we return to that terrace with poplars, the tables are still empty, it's like a movie set, we select a table in the shade, an unmemorable waiter materialises and takes our order, he brings a big silver pot of coffee, kaiser buns, soft-boiled eggs, white fluffy clouds cross a blue sky, this is happiness, I think, this is as good as it gets in life, Milena smiles, I reach under the table and squeeze her hand, her eyes water and she dabs them dry; apologises: Sorry, I'm just so happy, later we stroll along the main *Strasse* and over the railway crossing, we climb a narrow zig-zag road which rises steeply at the western end of the little town, heat shimmers from the road surface, the white Pensions dissolve into wobbly rectangles of colour, they are clustered closely together, the roof of one almost touching the garden wall of the one above it, alleyways curl off beside the houses, where white-haired figures doze on balconies, after half a mile the road forks, to our left it turns back to drop back down the mountainside in the form of a stretched-out Z, from here we can see the valley stretch away into the blue misty distance, with the toy spire rising from the next village, St Jakob, the church in St Anton is more distinctive, the dome is a golden hub, around which the village clusters, if you follow this valley far enough, Milena remarks, you will come eventually to Innsbruck and Vienna... Look, there are ski slopes nearby, green and snowless, dissected by the black wires which hold the chairlifts, framed by dark surges of forest, twenty minutes have passed since the lovers left their restaurant table, they take the right fork, where a narrower road goes on up the slope, half-constructed Pensions line the road in a surge of development, a signpost indicates a short-cut for walkers through a copse of pines and we leave the road behind, amid the trees the sunlight forms golden pools on a dense carpet of dead twigs and pine cones, a bird coos gently nearby as if admiring the stylish description which this scene merits, the air smells crisp and mint-fragrant, astonishingly, a little further on, there's an open-air swimming pool, it's set in a clearing, fenced off, surrounded by benches, there's no one in it, the water is startlingly blue, the wind-rippled surface reflects shimmering patterns along the edges, in a movie I suppose M and L would strip off and splash and dive and surface and laugh and afterwards copulate joyously amid the ferns, if there were any, but they did not, the foliage remained out of focus, beyond the pool they met the road again, another five minutes and we reach our destination, *Haus Pepi Eiter*, what in England would be called a bed-and-breakfast establishment, a middle-aged woman greets us at the door, I catch the brief flicker of surprise in her eyes at the sight of a young man and an older woman checking in together, we are required to hand her our passports, which expose this liaison, a married Canadian woman of forty-nine and an Englishman in his twenties, she says Pepi will take his car and collect our bags from the station, meanwhile Mrs E offers us coffee and a slice of fruit cake and we sit at a table in the garden at the rear of the Pension until he returns, we drink our coffee, saying little, we are both tired by the walk uphill under the blazing sun, soon Pepi returns, our room is spacious and clean and there is a view of the valley from the window, there is even a balcony, with even better views of St Anton and the mountains, plus, Louise, a complimentary small bar of the local chocolate, Milena runs a bath and we share it, gently soaping each other, then we go to bed and make love and afterwards fall asleep, did this really happen or have I invented it, I no longer know, perhaps there is a notebook entry somewhere which might clarify the matter, when we wake it is late afternoon, we walk into town, go to a bar for a drink, then on to a brasserie for a light supper, then back to *Haus Pepi Eiter* where we sit on a pair of rickety chairs on the balcony, it's nine and the great amber band of sunlight on the mountain opposite has risen higher and higher until at last it loses its colour and becomes extinguished among the highest grey ridges, she likes me to read to her so I go and get my paperback anthology of modern poetry, I read her Lawrence's poem about gentians: *torch-flower of the blue-smoking darkness, Pluto's dark-blue daze*, it's beautiful, she whispers, I read her 'Like The Touch of Rain' by Edward Thomas, I don't read her any more after this because when I look up she's quietly crying, I go across and take her hand and we go inside, I comfort her, Don't cry, I say, I can't help it, she says, such happiness as ours... it cannot last, this is like a movie, there should be violins, I take her in my arms, I brush my fingers lightly over her small body: breasts, bottom, crotch, gently I undo her shirt, I unclip the twin hooks of her black bra, I slide her yellow skirt off, I kneel and pull down her red knickers, I bury my face in her pubic hair, here we go again, you expect better from Ellis Sharp than erotica and a

83

plunge into Henry Miller territory, whose books brought the cops to Orwell's door, I kiss her mound, wait, she starts to unbutton my shirt, peels away my jeans and underpants, we stand face to face, nude, stomach to stomach, my erect penis presses against the tiny bulge of her tummy, I am too faaat, she smiles, apologetically, stretching out the word, nonsense, I go back to the windows and open them wide, I draw back the long lace curtains, outside the first bright stars shine in the deepening night, they mirror the twinkling lights of the little town far below, I go back and draw Milena down to the carpet, we explore each other's bodies, licking, touching, stroking... we fuck, afterwards we get into the big bed and hold each other, remember the Château, the time we almost got run down by that crazy driver just outside, madman, remember the deer by the Kyleakin ferry, everything, I remember everything, I did then but now no longer, the past is frayed and fraying, bits are flaking off like a disintegrating fuselage, the panels are ripped away, the horse chestnuts of the Lake District were once significant but now they have fallen and rotted into nothingness, we rush on through cold space but soon everything will fall apart, and then down we'll tumble, in the distance a remote tinkling begins, like chandeliers rattling in a sudden gust, it continues, it seems to be getting closer, Milena knows what it is, cattle, it's the herd, being brought in for the night, the clanking bells grow closer, closer, *bong-bong*, they go, *bong-bong*, someone not too far away shouts into the night, a wooden door is closed, and now the sound of the bells begins to thin and fade, ten minutes later the silence returns, Milena turns off the light, we fall asleep in each other's arms, Tell me more about your father, I say next morning, we are sitting on a little terrace where, if you wish, you can take your breakfast outside, another couple – plump, middle-aged – are already sat there, they nod a *Morgen* at us as we pass, through a brick arch can be seen a tiny courtyard containing four wooden hives, bees move in and out, intermittently a single fat bee passes sluggishly across the terrace, emitting a low whine, what about my father? about the camp, you've never really talked about it, the camp, Theresienstadt, or as a Czech patriot would say, to avoid the foul and repellent German language: Terezin, Milena is not a bitter woman, she uses the German name, besides, her mother was German, as a girl Militká had been brought up in the countryside outside Prague, her mother was German but her father was Czech, worse than that, he was a Jew, in 1942 – a little shrug – they came for him... he always said he would not tell us about the camp, I was only a girl then, but I found out anyway, she shivers, you see my mother and father sent me to stay with three aunts in Prague after the war ended, I went to a Catholic school, and one of the aunts had been in Auschwitz, and she never stopped telling me about it, a bitter woman, she loathed Germans, and Theresienstadt? oh, stupid things, silly things, the commandant made the women form a choir, to sing carols at Christmas, he sang a duet with a contralto, from *Don Giovanni*, even those poor prisoners wept, then two days later he had her shot, why, why did he do that, a whim, she sang better than he did, and those women, were they ever... touched by the guards, rape? never, the Germans were very strict about that, a guard would have been executed for that, silence as a waitress brings a silver pot of hot coffee, two freshly baked kaiser buns with the cross pressed into the crust, two boiled eggs, and a saucer of lime marmalade, there was one thing he told me, years later, about the day he entered the camp, the twenty new prisoners were ordered to squat on the ground, they were then told to hop up a grassy slope on the camp perimeter, as they hopped five of them were shot, but not my father, he was spared because he was married to an Aryan, a strange ethics, she smiles sadly:

Enough of this doom and gloom, she pronounces it *ee-nuff* and *dumb* and *glum*, the written word never catches the voice, never, never, never, we spend a week in St Anton, we follow the mountain trails, marked by small boulders splashed with red paint, I am startled by all the wooden shrines, they are everywhere, a wooden Christus to mark every tragedy, a boy who drowned in a mountain torrent, a man killed in a hunting accident, and those huge crosses on the mountain peaks, vaguely sinister, it's as if the crucifixion happened only the previous month, or perhaps they simply remind me of the end of *Spartacus*, one bright sunlit afternoon, when we were high up a grassy mountain slope, there was a noise like a sudden clap of thunder, for a moment I wondered if a bomb had gone off, but then Milena pointed and explained, she was a teacher after all, it was an avalanche, on the far side of the valley, weakened by the summer heat a vast sheet of ice and snow had come loose somewhere up near the crest, it crashed down the mountain and hit a belt of pine trees, a white surge of something resembling smoke rose up from the point of impact, then it died away and everything became the picture of tranquillity again, next day we climbed up to the Edelhütte, as a little girl I could not understand the devil's temptation of Christ she said, what would anyone *do* with all that land? I am tempted by another possibility, I whisper in her ear, here, I nod, she looks down the mountain, no sign of any walkers approaching, when it is over she moves her head back and smiles up at me, her eyes light up with merriment, caviar! she shrieks, did that happen, did I imagine it, I am on the borderlands, the past, the mountain mist, she remembers the Muirs, pioneer translators of Kafka, I look at my crumbling copy of *Das Schloss* and there they are, Willa and Edwin, their first translation of this work appearing in 1930, with an Introduction by Edwin remarking that Franz Kafka's name 'so far as I can discover, is almost unknown to English readers', adding that the Czech's work was 'strange' and 'disconcerting', a translation first appearing as a Penguin Book in 1957, under the auspices of the British Council the Muirs staged plays at the British Consulate in Prague, Milena remembers appearing in a dramatisation of a Jane Austen novel, she was twenty, she played a maid, she had a seven-word speaking part, she remembers it to this day, enter stage left: tea is served in the green room, exit, this is what it all amounts to, n'est-ce pas Louise? performances, farewells, She had a light, clever, familiar way of traversing an imm-ense distance with a very few words wrote Henry James in *The Bostonians*, one day we walk to St Jakob, where do you think he is now? I ask, she doesn't need to ask who I mean by *he*, she lets the question drift, in the end she says: I don't know, still in Johannesburg, I suppose, let's not talk about him, at St Jakob Milena wants to go inside the church, the baroque extravagance of the interior offends my subliminal English Protestant sensibility, that chubby devil and crude zig-zag lightning, the wooden life-size tortured Christ, the memorial photos of Austrian soldiers, who froze to death on the Russian front, the dates after 1945 of the ones who died of sickness and malnutrition in Russian camps, the monument to the sixty-six Italian workers – my God, *sixty-six*! – who died building the Arlberg tunnel, in this place of shining gilt and death various candles burn, and in a dark corner like a watchful waiting spider stands a black-robed lanky priest, his white bony face nods coldly in our direction, I am glad to be out of that place, we walk in the woods, we come to a waterfall, *Die wasserfall*, it is the colour of milk, water streams down from the great ribbed glaciers high at the end of the tributary valleys, cold and pure as Kafka's prose, a late addition to the text Louise, back in St Anton there's a sudden foul stench rising from a manhole cover in the main street, a week of walking, talking and fucking, she's the most sexually charged woman I've ever known, no pun, she contorts with ecstasies, it is sex beyond language, beyond mere words, Christ this sounds trite, it's a week when the sun shines unceasingly, the words are lovely dark and deep, a slip only spotted later, and then it is over, *bong-bong*, on our last day in St Anton we went for a final walk along a mountain path, against spectacular scenery – *bong-bong* – she described to me the plot of *Homo Faber*, a novel by the Zurich-born novelist Max Frisch, you should read it, she urged, I will, I said, when I get back to London I will buy a copy, and now this week is over and we are back at the station St Anton-am-Arlberg to catch the identical express train reminding me of that opening page to Chapter X where the Consul recalls fair-haired angelic Lee Maitland who he had gone to meet light-headed light-footed on a platform a train of thought leading him to a memory of the delicious smell of onion soup in side-streets of Vavin meaning I suppose the Métro station and surely to thoughts of Jan but this time we continue on, eastwards, to Innsbruck, the mountains press closer as the valley narrows, at Innsbruck we change trains, for Munich, at Munich the weather changes, clouds the colour of a bruise pile up above the sultry, sticky heat of the city, we take a room at a characterless forgotten hotel near the railway station, Room 24, in Munich there are shop windows displaying the new Rolling Stones LP, *Black and Blue*, that summer's album, years later I discover that the Rolling Stones began recording the album at the Musicland Studios in Munich, a city where on the first Friday in July she buys me *Brockhaus-Bildwörterbücher in Zwei Sprachen*, a brick-sized illustrated German-English dictionary, and later she gives me a photocopy of a poem she once wrote, it's the only poem she's ever written, it was inspired by a nun she met in Spain thirteen years earlier, in her cell the nun had her own coffin, it was a *memento mori* and tool for meditation, Milena was overwhelmed by this strange encounter, 'Spanien' the poem was titled, Aus der bröcke / ligen Glut / der Sonne Spaniens / trat ich in kühle blaue Klostermauern. / Das feuchte Leben floss in mich zurück / mein Blut sang / es summten meine Sinne – / Bis / die kleine schwarze Nonne / kindlich schäkernd mir zeigte / mit rundem schwarzem Schuh /wo sie ruhen würde / unter der alten Steinfliesse / später / bald, Munich is a cursed city I feel, as overwrought as my later recording words, it holds Hitler's ghost, plus it is where Milena has to meet up with her husband, he is jetting in from South Africa, and I must be gone before that happens, the clock is ticking, the shadows are lengthening, the clichés are massing, I have been so happy Milena said that sometimes I wish I could fly away from all this and be done with the future, before then I say I want to see the concentration camp at Dachau, I feel I ought to, and it isn't far, because she's Jewish she isn't enthusiastic but she agrees, she'll do whatever I want her to, we walk to the main railway station which is only five minutes' walk from our hotel, we descend gleaming silver escalators to the new Underground system and find a route map, it resembles the elaborate cluster of interlocking lines of the London Underground, at the outer rim of this cluster, innocent as, is the station we are looking for, there, see, it's a shock when the conductor whispers the name over the train's intercom, next stop Dachau, *Dachau*, spoken in a soft tone, as casually as if the name was Morden or Burnt Oak or Walthamstow Central, a single-decker bus waits outside Dachau station to take the tourists there, K/Z a sign reads on a white card propped against the windscreen, six chattering American students board with us, as soon as we move off the driver takes the ash-white card down and puts it near his feet, the citizens of Dachau do not wish to be reminded, at the camp gate Milena flinches, she becomes

89

tearful, I cannot do this, I cannot go in, you go, I wait for you, she indicates a roadside café, it has tables outside, I wait there, go, please, she pushes me away, so I go, Dachau began as a factory, it still looks like one, I later buy an English language guide, useful when the internet does not yet exist, on 21 March 1933 the *Völkischer Beobachter* reported that a new kind of prison has been established at Dachau, with a capacity of 5,000, here all Communist Party officials and, as far as the security of the State requires, those of the 'Reichsbanner' and of the Social Democrats will be interned, a bleak collection of sheds under a grey sky, the Americans have vanished, I have the place to myself, I go inside one of the huts and I'm stunned to see rows of white china lavatories, they are not connected, but it can't have been like this, I think, this is a travesty, the hut has been reconstructed; it's not original, I go outside again and walk past a line of huts, they stir a dark memory of seeing Jakob Bronowski in an episode of *The Ascent of Man* suddenly reaching down to scoop up black, dripping mud, in the little visitor centre no one speaks English but there are signs for tourists like me who don't read German, they talk about Hitler coming to power in a coup, but I know that's not true, Hitler was elected, I buy two postcards, yes, they sell concentration camp postcards, having a nice time in Germany, wish you were here, I buy the English-language visitor booklet, which has the odd title *What was it like in the Concentration Camp at Dachau?* it contains ten photographs, none shows any corpses or skeletal prisoners, outside Milena is sitting drinking 7-Up under a big colourful table umbrella that bears the word MARTINI, she looks up, her voice sounds cracked, was it what you expected, not really, somehow I expected... more, it's strange but I don't feel anything, it's a lack of feeling rather than the emotions I suppose I should be feeling, want another drink, she shakes her head, I need a beer, a lorry passes, trailing a ribbon of blue fumes, inside the café a slutty-looking woman is leaning her elbows on the greasy counter, chatting to three truck-driver types, they scowl at my entrance, the scowls deepen when they hear my English accent, I order a beer, the jukebox is playing *Iche hab' noch einen Koffer in Berlin*, the song seems vaguely familiar but I'm probably just imagining I've heard it before, I made a note but not enough, this is the end, one ending anyroads, she recedes, tearfully waving, it's a long lonely night journey from Munich to Calais, a dismal Channel crossing, sunk in an imitation leather chair in the public lounge of a lurching Sealink ferry back to Dover I try to read *Anna Karenin* but it's hopeless, a colour TV booms a documentary about England, land of royal palaces, ancient castles, and an acquisitive double-chinned balding man who wrote plays, years later I read Gary Taylor's demolition of a man who accommodated himself to the values of his age, who dramatized the daydreams of his culture, who delivered softness, mushiness, wholesomeness, who became a black hole warping cultural space-time, we're back to palaces, teenagers run around being teenagerish, grannies yelp for more tea and another chocolate biscuit, a blur of boredom and angst carries me back to Finchley past Kent scrapyards, the fall of rain, the interminable suburban wastes of outer London, I miss her, I miss her smile, her twinkling eyes, her conversation, life had a burning intensity in her presence, now all I have is dead words and fading Polaroids, the room is lifeless without her, I sit on the broken sofa and feel the sagging springs flatten out beneath me, I look at the faded orange curtains, so old that the fabric is beginning to flake off, I make myself a cup of tea on the tiny two-ring Baby Belling electric cooker, just one letter is waiting for me on my return, it's from Smorg, he's written a book about rein-carnation, now all he has to do is find a publisher, he is still under the impression he can convert L to his own crackpot obsessions, I have heard from a very interesting American who has used infra-red film to photograph biological entities in space he writes, some look like UFO patterns, I think he is on to something, the pictures were taken in California, about 5,000 feet up, from a mountain top at dawn, remember L that all extensions to the human senses (telescopes, microscopes etc.) are merely registering effects of unknowns, i.e. these instrument readings are then interpreted by the human mind and a belief-system which is defective, Smorg, PS The Souvenir Press has sent me a card to say that they have received my manuscript entitled *Forgotten Dreams? Forgotten Lives?* next day I received an airmail letter from Canada, I didn't recognise the handwriting, it was from a friend of Irish Jack, who'd found my name and address in Jack's notebook, Jack was dead, the narrative had no further use for him, it was necessary to wrap things up in a satisfactory manner for the benefit of the reader's sleep and possible future discussion at a reading group, Irish Jack was run down (multiple ironies) by a drunk motorist on Granville, outside the hotel where I'd once lived, the driver's name was Charlie Dickinson, it was a terrific shock, I raised some alcohol to Irish Jack's memory, in truth I barely remember him now, I never think of him, the day after that, restless, I went into the city, I sat in a café off Charlotte Street drinking thin watery coffee, the plastic table was sticky, flies flickered by, feasting on crumbs, the waitress, a girl of about fifteen, came round the tables, ladling out sugar with a china cup which she kept dipping into a plastic washing-up bowl, welcome back to England, next day an airmail letter from Germany: Darling, darling L, I am having lunch, alone, a salad with wine à la Viennese, I see you everywhere throughout Munich, wherever I walk, be it the Neuhauser Street, American Express, post office or station, and I hear your voice and I can't stop thinking of you for more than one minute, how did you travel, my darling? I do hope you slept and were not too exhausted, I followed your journey in my mind all day yesterday, I took the train to a little village and walked through fields and villages, it was hot but I was glad to be able to walk because I felt very restless and... but need I tell you? I know you know, no news yet except two cards from South Africa, Waclaw will be arriving shortly, I will be strong, I don't know whether you feel my thoughts and love around you, somehow I think you must, I feel yours, I will write soon again, I kiss you and hold you and kiss you, your Milena, on the second Tuesday in July, marking the letter 11am, she wrote my darling, Waclaw arrived last night over an hour late and quite tired and it was impossible to talk then, I picked up your letter this morning – thank you, my Love, I, too, find no words to tell you how I feel, I am upset but I will talk as soon as possible, we left the Pension early and are going to the Black Forest this afternoon, I can't see my way beyond an hour – my thoughts are not in Munich but with you, you will hear from me soon – as soon as I can, forgive me for torturing you, I am terribly tortured myself, I hold you and kiss you my love, my darling, M, and then the third Friday in July, My Love, I had much mail from you yesterday, two letters which made me ache with feeling – your pain merged with mine – they seemed to embrace and hold each other, I must not upset you and me, I wish I had some music to listen to, the other day I managed to play 'Sailing' on a jukebox in a bar where I had gone for lemonade, I am so incapable of thinking clearly when I read your letters, I cherish every word you write, your walk through Parliament Hill, I have been wondering why that particular walk impressed itself so strongly on our minds and memories, we have taken so many walks but somehow that one carried within itself an abandon hard to put into words, do you understand what I mean, my Love, I should know more about the future by Monday, Waclaw has proofs here, he must finish them first and the publisher has made the mistake of using American spelling in the manuscript, so now it must be changed and Waclaw has a lot of work with it, the past two days I have gone for a morning walk, the woods are fragrant and cool and I saw six deer and three hares, thank God, I think the knowledge that we will see each other soon gives us something to hold on to, my Love, my Love, M, she returned to me, after a week with Waclaw who had returned to Vancouver, she made excuses not to go with him, she told him she had to go to London to do some research at the British Library, he accepted this, he never seemed bothered by all the time she was spending away from him, like the base Indian, threw a pearl away richer than all his tribe, she said Waclaw hadn't had sex with her, hard to believe, he'd been away from her for weeks, his balls must have been at bursting point, I fucked her three times in a row, trying to prove something, she was as greedy for sex as I was, our days were numbered, a new term was starting, we only had five days, the nights were hot and heavy that ultra-hot summer, we were soaked in sweat, sometimes, lying on top of her, our stomachs would become glued together, pulling apart after sex required surprising energy and effort, our stomachs parted reluctantly, making a sharp, protracted, squelching noise, we went out, at the National Gallery we stared at pictures, the one I remember most is Bronzino's 'Venus, Cupid, Folly and Time', this highly-charged erotic canvas is where the estranged lovers meet and reconcile in *The Nice and the Good*, only connect, we took a trip on the Thames, from Westminster to Greenwich and back, afterwards we wandered beside the Thames, a band in Embankment Gardens was playing a haunty piece by Janáček, *jaunty* I meant to write but *haunty* is a good word I think, sparrows hopped on the baked ground and raised puffs of dust, where have all the sparrows gone? we stood on the steps below Cleopatra's Needle, in the dark choppy water an object slowly drifted into view, it washed closer, a cylindrical object which glittered, Milena flinches, she sees it's a dead fish, silver-scaled, she squeezes my hand, a wave larger than the others tips the dead fish over on to the wet step below, its eyes are grey and unseeing, then another wave takes it back into the river, we watch it bob away, in the direction of Gravesend, she embraces me, in Highgate we followed in the footsteps of two famous English poets, up a narrow lane where from the open window of a house a record player was loudly playing Fairport Convention's 'Si Tu Dois Partir', all this really happened, there should have been a film crew, a crane, microphones, we went to Keats's house, I remember almost nothing about it, a tree in the garden perhaps, the nightingale, we walked across Hampstead Heath, we drank at Jack Straw's Castle, we drank at the King of Bohemia, 10 Hampstead High Street, that place was special, Hugh remembers that the last time he ever played his guitar was in this pub, pseudo-American twanging he calls his musical ability, not even good twanging, Hugh recalls he drank too much and passed out, when he regained consciousness the pub was full of his friends singing 'Oh, clear away the track and let the bulgine run', on our final morning we took a taxi to the station, she had so much baggage this woman, the mountain ash which lined the street was in crimson bloom, that last Thursday in August, an unforgettable, heart-piercing, terrible date, at Heathrow we embraced one final time and then she was through the security gate, I turned away and left, hurriedly, there's a worse date to follow, I wept that day, I wept on the coach back to Victoria Station, I wept in the streets of London as I stumbled blindly around and eventually made my way back to that little room in Finchley, the bed without her was like a tomb, I was cold as Romeo, in the days – the daze – that followed like a corpse in a Dennis Wheatley occult tale I went back to all the places we'd been, a ghost still caught by agony's suction to a life that had been lived, an attachment to what had once occurred, a specific point on a grassy slope on Hampstead Heath, a café on Villiers Street, a particular corner table in The Lamb and Flag, there was even a point at the foot of the escalators at Tottenham Court Road tube station that held her shimmering presence for many years until the bastards modernised the station and exorcised it, day after burning day passed, a week went by before I received her first letter, written on thin blue airmail paper on her flight back to Vancouver, she had written it at one in the afternoon, she was over the Atlantic, Darling L (wrote darling M), My Love, here I sit drinking gin and tonic, My Love, my Love, my Love, I am so full of your presence that my eyes keep brimming over and I hear your voice in my ears and feel your hands on my body and all the words I say express only a minute fraction of what I feel, I have thought a thousand times that I am the luckiest woman under the sun because you love me, I once told you that I always waited for something during these past years, and at the same time I thought and said to myself: Don't be stupid, life consists of irrational feelings and expectations and you are an unrealistic fool as a child or a naïve woman outstaring life and its relentless earthy laws, and then YOU stepped into my life and when an unknown power made me touch your face, my fingers felt as if they had touched an inexplicable region to which I was drawn, when I left you that day I held my hand to my own face (I never told you that) and I ran down the library stairs with my heart beating in my ears, where are you now, my Love question mark, perhaps at number 44 question mark or in the park question mark or walking along a street in London which has proportions for me now that I never dreamt of question mark, I followed you with my eyes when you walked away through the crowd and I wanted to run after you and hold you and then people pushed me in... All I could think of then was the moment when *I* will see *you* emerging from a door or a crowd, she wrote, but that imaginary scene never occurred, I was left alone with the last chapter, Diosdado (a fine name, Louise!) suddenly slaps a fat package of envelopes fastened with elastic down on to the bar, and so off we go, again and again and again, into that inner room, one of the boxes in the Chinese puzzle, a room in the same continuum as to be found in the house of Mrs Eleanor Bull of Deptford perhaps, with a barman named Sherlock, and did you know Coriolanus is dead question mark, muddle muddle muddle, fetch me a glass of port, water, three paracetamol, My Love, I am disjointed and my thoughts whirl through my head Milena wrote, one thing I know: that my love for you is rooted in my heart for as long as I breathe, I have lived so long (relatively speaking) but I have such a feeling as if I realized only now the nature of love or life – God knows, I cover my eyes in the palm of my hand – and I see you before me – and I feel you inside me and I feel the sweetness of your skin under my fingertips, Milena's words, what is there in life besides the person whom one adores and the life one can build with that person question mark, Yvonne's words, Lowry's words, Jan's words I suppose, I pick up her book, yes, he looted her letters, on January 5 Jan wrote: *I wrote again, the week had been a nightmare, My love, my love, ellipses, do you remember tomorrow, question mark,* My Love, wrote Milena, once when you are in the mood, will you tell me why you think we love each other so, the three levels we talked about (intellect, emotion and Eros) are OK but I want to know more, exclamation mark, if you like I will tell you too but my words would be so awkward and grotesque messengers of my feelings, such style, such passion, L goes back to the Farolito, my heart has the taste of ashes Yvonne wrote, Jan wrote *Malc excerpted portions of my letter with the caustic query: 'had Yvonne been reading Héloïse and Abélard?'*, Milena wrote But *you* tell me exclamation mark and, since we both love irony and basically grin at emotional wallowing, tell me ironically, with salt on your words and a bright searching spotlight on your feelings (excuse mixed image exclamation mark), I am so thirsty for all that concerns you and us exclamation mark and if I shrugged my shoulders last night at the pub in Hampstead (the first one, near Keats's house) when you told me it would not make any sense to tell me about Honey Maddox I was lying a bit, actually I would very much like to know exactly what your feelings were for that woman, whether it was a deep passion or an intoxication or whether she was just *there* with her blonde hair and sensual limbs for you to touch and enflame yourself against, Malcolm Lowry was angry with Jan when he wrote that final chapter but later it seems to me he became intoxicated by her memory and I wonder if Margerie ever spotted the significance of that title using Gabriola, I suspect not, I don't think either of the two wives were attuned to irony like Lowry was, always befuddled about my letters (grumbled Jan), scanned boozily and left behind in bars, small wonder he reconstructed their contents so haphazardly, I want your happiness beneath my heart and your sorrows in my eyes and your peace in the fingers of my hand wrote Yvonne-Jan, I don't talk as a jealous woman, I know she is in the past and the present is ours – yours and mine – and *no one* can match that, but I wonder and think so much about you that I feel I must tell you the truth about wanting to know about you, wrote Milena, I think I only fathom now what wanting to possess the past of your lover means, and yet the word jealousy is wrong, I have such a serene feeling about our love that I just smile or whatever, I must stop this wrote Milena, luckily lunch came round and I *had* to stop exclamation mark, I think of our delicious first evening meal and of last night's equally delicious Schnitzl, my darling Ell I did not even thank you for my final glorious week in London, I was so confused and dazed and lightheaded this morning that I hardly knew what I was saying and doing, the Consul stood up, Yvonne had certainly been reading *something* Malcolm Lowry wrote, odd how a work of fiction can precede reality, a distant breaking of thunder, we must both work now like fury to bridge this terrible separation Milena wrote, I hope, my Love, you have the strength to make it, I did, I did, but you did not, to continue: but you will, you will Milena wrote, and then we can be free for what we really want to do, I wish I could be with you all the time, our love-making is such a glorious miracle, where would he find her now wonders the Consul, a girl turns a succession of cartwheels on the lush plot, everyone is laughing, miserably he wanted Yvonne and did not want her, it is always clever to trick your voices is it not Louise, under a brilliant full moon a stag stood by a river down which a man and a woman were paddling a birch bark canoe, the calendar was set to the future, he heard his voices again, the evening was filled with odd noises like those of sleep, it might have been a solution to return there but now too at least this much was clear, 6.30pm London time, Darling L, I just saw part of a pretty awful film exclamation mark with Walter Matthau as an aging unemployed enter-tainer, I was not at all in the mood for it and closed my eyes half the time, now I am listening to Mozart arias on the tape and reading a selection of English poetry, tell me, my Love, which of the following poets you think are good – just give me a couple of adjectives with each name: Enright, Davie, Larkin (we talked about him), Blackburn, Gunn, Tomlinson,

Geoffrey Hill, he laughed once more, feeling a strange release, his mind was clear as he re-read what she'd written long ago, he felt free to devour what remained, Sylvia Plath, Milena wrote, has a poem 'Mirror' which sustains the image beautifully, I get the volume down, I read the poem, year after year after year has passed, in the long aftermath I even went to Plath's grave, I have always enjoyed graveyards, hers was unkempt, hard to find, monstrous Hughes had neglected its maintenance, the name carved there – three words – a name she never was, a day I remember well, I was married by then, I took my wife with me, in Heptonstall we had to dodge back into a doorway to avoid a lout on his tractor, speeding, he looked about fourteen, the soot-black stone of the houses, a dismal place, even amidst fierce flames etcetera, I am not cruel only truthful, of course, Milena wrote, it is plathlike gloomy, L, L, I want so much to read more of what you have read, I have learned a great deal from you already, the captain just said that we will land in Calgary in just over an hour, the flight went *very* quickly exclamation, I have not at all the feeling that I have moved far away from you, the feeling that I can jump on a plane and be with you ten hours later is very important to me, if it didn't cost so much I could do it over a long weekend, My Love, I have feelings more deeply than I can tell you, but one thing is certain, we will be together soon and we will talk and share all our thoughts and anguishes and hopes, and we will give each other strength by our presence because our love is like a light that shines through all the storms of life, yes, no, never never never, she rewards me with tears and an agitation of hands, she comes and goes (how true!), I am in your hands now, save – The Consul looked up, pocketing his letters, it is the last chapter of the last and second novel Malcolm Lowry will publish in his lifetime, in the United States on 19 February 1947, Lowry died on 27 June 1957, aged forty-seven, by this time *Under the Volcano* was out of print in the United States and Britain, Janine outlived him by fifty-four years, *Gabriola* ends with a man looking for a new home on an obscure island, the woman who offers guidance on the island is Angela d'Arrivee, the light is fading and the prospect is of a sheltered valley that slopes down to a silent, calm harbour, Shangri-La or death or both perhaps, another airmail envelope arrives, I tear it open, inside is a postcard of Vancouver, an aerial shot, on the back of it Milena has written: *He's found out*, her signature is as shaky as the one at the end of tortured Guido Fawkes's confession, next day another airmail envelope arrives, My Love, I feel restless and agitated, Waclaw is so pale and his hands are shaking, he was told by a colleague he had seen me kissing you, this was some months ago, Waclaw dismissed the idea, he was told by another colleague she had seen me in Gastown with a young man, he was unsure, he said nothing, he bottled it up, he could not believe I would be unfaithful to him – least of all with you, he knew we were both at the library, he continues to call you 'the boy', upon his return he was told by a neighbour that a young man had been to the apartment in his absence, on many occasions, once, she told him, she saw something which she should not have seen, you see, the curtain was not fully drawn that night, he told me these things, he asked me directly, I told him, Yes, Yes, I am in love, I cannot help myself, he broke down, he wept, since then he stares at me as if I was a stranger to him, a third airmail envelope arrives, the final one, O my darling, my darling L, I want to write about literature and my feelings for you and my pain which is great and my hopes which I hold almost physically with my hands pressed against my heart but I won't write any more today, nothing good will come out, I can feel that, my sweet love, what is this life in which one plagues oneself so and in which one's strongest feelings are bound, I am surrounded with objects from you, they have become my most precious possessions, O my Love, I haven't heard your voice for so long, forgive this disjointed scribble, I will write better soon, I hold out my face for you to kiss, will you kiss it? will you hold me? I know nothing about the hours of each day of your life now, I know nothing, that is very hard to bear, Your beloved Milena xxx, then silence, nothing but silence, you must remember there were no computers then, no email, and in those days there were only two ways to make a telephone call, one required a landline, with a device attached to a miserably short length of curly plastic cord, or you could walk out along the street to the nearest red telephone box, letters to and from the rabbit-hole took anything from six to ten days to travel to their destination, and there are no further letters, on the fourth morning I can't hold back, I telephone her apartment, even though I know Waclaw may be the one who answers, I am a soul in agony, in a red London telephone box, *dring-dring, dring-dring*, no answer, I press Button B and start again, again and again, again and again, *dring-dring, dring-dring*, no answer, never any answer, never, never, never, never, an impatient middle-aged man with a moustache is rapping irritably on the smeared glass door, his cheeks are red, his mouth opens and twists (Go away Moustache!), I haven't got all day, he shouts, go away pest, go away, where are you my love? why don't you ever answer the phone? why no letters? almost two months have passed and this hot unforgettable summer is approaching its end, on the crowded platform of the station for Kursk can be seen the famous Count Vronsky, the platform is crowded with volunteers who are off to Serbia to fight against the Turks, Vronsky is going with them, in the circumstances it is the best thing he can do, he has even raised a group of fighters, financed at his own expense, a kind of atonement, perhaps, after *his misfortune*, what else is there for him to do? for six weeks afterwards he barely ate, he retreated from the world, speaking to no one, he was like one dead, prostration complete, raving mad almost, the Serbian war is a blessing, it distracts his mind, and to add to his other miseries he is suffering from toothache, see here he comes! Count Vronsky strides towards the train with his mother on his arm, she is the only one there to see him off, he is wearing a long overcoat and broad-brimmed black hat, at his side is Oblonsky, who is here by chance, Oblonsky merrily babbles away, Vronsky is frowning and looking straight ahead, his mind elsewhere, Oblonsky must have said something to to him for now he turns in the direction of two aquaintances who are standing watching, Vronsky raises his hat but says nothing, his face, aged and full of suffering, looks like stone, reaching the train Vronsky lets his mother board before him, silently he disappears with her into one of the compartments, she is going with him as far as Kursk, the Count pulls the blind down, shortly afterwards whistles blow, the locomotive belches its first deep-throated bolt of steam, the big wheels turn and the great train begins to roll out of the station, at Tsaritsyno station there is a choir on the platform, it is made up of young men, they are there to greet the volunteers with a rousing patriotic song, at the next big station it's the same: the train is greeted with patriotic songs and cheering, and now the train halts in the principal town of the province, Vronsky gets out to stretch his legs, he strides up and down, writes Tolstoy, like a caged animal, the Count is approached by Sergei Ivanovich Koznyshev, who has something of a reputation as an intellectual, Koznyshev's book, six years in the writing, has only recently been published, it's a work of political science – an analysis of the principles and forms of governance in Europe and Russia, with quiet expectation Koznyshev has waited to see its impact on society (how L knows that feeling!), but its publication has been ignored, weeks passed without a single review (again like L!), then finally a young journalist reviewed it, the review was a savage hatchet-job which selected a variety of quotations to claim that Koznyshev was an ignoramus and his book merely an accumulation of pretentious rhetoric, why is it that Koznyshev reminds me so strongly of Professor W. C. Slabczynski? and why is it that this fiercely sarcastic young reviewer reminds me of my younger self? Koznyshev realises he is intruding on this distracted, restless man but he wants to congratulate Vronsky on his support for a great cause, Vronsky stares at him, recognises him, shakes his hand, he smiles with his lips only, writes Tolstoy, the Count's eyes are full of bitter suffering, to make matters worse he is still suffering from that corrosive and enduring toothache, Vronsky's jaw is in constant motion, trying to shake off the pain, now a train approaches, the Count stares at its approaching wheels, he had first met Anna Karenin at a station, how mysterious and exquisite she had seemed back then! and what a lover she had become, bestowing him with kisses and happiness, Vronsky wrenches himself from these memories and holds a quick, terse conversation with Koznyshev about the conflict, politics can always distract you from matters of the heart, not least in a pandemic, and then the second bell rings and they return to their own train to continue the journey, and life goes on, pitiful banal magical wonderful life always goes on, no matter who departs – whether Presidents, novelists or the great love of your life – Anna Karenin dies on page 802 but afterwards there are another 51 pages, Koznyshev arrives at the Pokrovskoe house accompanied by Katavasov, Kitty feeds her baby, Levin wrestles with ethics and the meaning of life, a little green beetle crawls up a stalk of couch-grass, it finds its route blocked by a leaf of goutwort, in the south the sky is clear but in the other direction there is distant thunder and flashes of lightning, raindrops drip from the lime trees, the comfort of house guests must be attended to, goodness must be sought in life, and somewhere, out there in the night, Vronsky is arriving at the front, he feels his life has no value, he has sufficient energy to hurl himself at what awaits him, he will beat on through or fall and be destroyed, it's all the same to him, she died, two words suffice, this is the end of the story, Milena died, I have waited so long to say this, that fall she fell, in the not-long-after-our-separation, when the first brittle yellow leaves were beginning to drop from the trees, when summer ended and the days grew colder, and this is how it is, there is a place where some of us – many of us – spend our lives, it is in the aftermath of a great event, and if, as Marx famously remarked, history repeats itself the first time as tragedy and the second time as farce, my own titillating text must surely sullenly partake of both – the low comedy of searching for an absence – a peat-stained phantom – an entity present in the first draft, then deleted – is matched by the loss of Milena, of a narrative that would never be written, an abortion which left an ache, a melo-dramatic scar every bit as good as Harry Potter's, which no amount of sex, drugs or alcohol could ever numb, or to put it another way there were five more days of silence and then an airmail envelope, my name and address typed on it, inside was a short press cutting, nothing else, an anonymous communication, a friend of Milena's who did not wish to be involved? Waclaw himself? I never found out, **Professor Dies in Fall**, the headline, and below: Tributes have been paid to Professor Militká Slabczynski, 49, who has died after falling from her eighth-floor office in the Department of English building on campus, head of department Glen Green said that there was a deep sense of shock among staff, 'She was a popular member of our team who will be missed terribly', he said, police say foul play is not suspected, more anonymous cuttings followed, the first reported her funeral, the others the inquest, a thudding succession of facts and illumination, always sent in envelopes with my name and address typed, never handwritten, the verdict was that it was just a tragic accident, the Professor had been reaching out to close an open window when she'd slipped and fallen through the gap, death was instantaneous, her husband who had been with her at the time described what had happened, the police exonerated him from any responsibility for what was just a tragic accident, I didn't believe it, the bastard pushed her, he was a liar, he told the inquest that he and his wife had a very strong marriage and were very much in love with each other, no, there were no difficulties inside his marriage, none whatsoever, and then I remembered John Fowles's brilliant phantasmagorical novel *The Magus*, the hero, Nicholas Urfe, is tricked into thinking that his lover is dead, but she isn't, Urfe has to be taught a harsh lesson in appreciating someone he has taken for granted and whose trust he has abused, so perhaps all these press cuttings were fake, it was all just a diabolical trick on Waclaw's part to silence me and punish me, then I remembered Rabbit-Hole House in London, Milena had once told me that the main Rabbit-Hole newspapers were on display there each day, for anyone who cared to walk in and read them, I went there and checked, it didn't take me very long to find out that the cuttings were genuine, I walked out and across Trafalgar Square, tears pouring down my cheeks, I found out the address of the relevant Rabbit-Hole police HQ, I sent an anonymous letter informing them that Milena had been having a torrid affair with a young student, her husband had found out shortly before her mysterious fall, perhaps they should investigate the possibility that he had murdered her, this letter must have gone straight into the bin, for nothing ever happened, the career of Professor W. C. Slabczynski thrived, he published two more works of political science, in his little world he was as big as Abe Ravelstein, he never remarried, he died of cancer the day after 9/11, could I have done more? should I have done more? should I have dropped back into the rabbit-hole? not easy, my visa to Wonderland had expired, I had no money, plus I was blind with grief and loss, and perhaps the cops were right all along, maybe it *was* just a tragic accident, or perhaps – probably – it was what no one really wanted to admit, her death was self-inflicted, deliberate, a wild foolish impulsive gesture to hurt Waclaw, and me, in her agony she had once hinted at this solution, in some suicides the pain is sharpened to a point which becomes a desire to hurt those perceived to be responsible for the sufferer's overwhelming despair, I remembered the time, quite early on in our affair, when Milena once told me of a colleague who'd stopped her one day in the Safeway supermarket on West 10th, he'd also originated from Eastern Europe, he'd looked at her in an odd way, she remembered, are you at home here, Milena? he asked, his name was Franz, a Wonderland coincidence (for Wonderland like any modern novel is full of coincidence and twistings), bewildered she'd replied instaneously: But yes, Yes, of course, Yes, I am at home in Wonderland, although when I think about it more she had a strange passion for Unica Zürn, and Franz had shrugged, a rare case of a clichéd narrative spasm becoming actually existing, and Franz walked off, three days later he threw himself from the top floor of the new arts building, so it goes, *Well, I should think you could do with a drink after that*, yes please, thanks, the news of her death and burial broke me, I entered a dark, self-destructive phase of my life, alcohol, drugs, a woman or two, a flat-chested one with lines down her cheeks and a taste for the unusual, a voluptuous big-breasted gal with a strangely elongated form, very fit, which she put to excellent use, they need not concern you Louise, this book, Louise, is neither an inventory nor a boast,

I am broken inside and in time I shall die, as will we all, as will you my old friend, as will the reader, farewell, it's been good to know you, to share this tiny yet expansive space with you, I say this simply to explain that though the reckoning was great I managed to totter out of the death room, out of the operating theatre, out of all the lonely cold bedsits, I staggered on, in due course I discovered the existence of Henry Parrot the epigrammatist and John Penkethman author of books about the price of bread who described himself as *a publike writer* and John Bale's volume of biographies of English writers with the entry *Miles Pig: His father's name is said to be Hoggard but I call him Pig because he was a sodomistic papistical pig, he wrote many dirty verses against the true religion, and died to the great thanksgiving of many*, a style of biography now alas entirely out of fashion, at times I even managed to whistle Lillibullero and once, twice, I went to Coxwold, I paid my respects, I bought the best annotated edition I could find, outside it was starting to snow, I managed to sparkle, though I was cold and scorched and everything was ash, later, after many stirring adventures, like a John Buchan hero or someone with a pot of porridge, I came through, unlike D. H. Lawrence I will not invite you to look, unlike Humpty Dumpty I was put back together again, 'Your hair was darker, then', 'My heart was lighter, then', yes, yes indeedy, these are the memoirs of a survivor but I would have you know there is a crack running through me, I have a fine sheer breakage, cleverly concealed, I am glued back into one piece, as Dolly says I'll think of you each step of the way but then again as Waylon says I'll live to see it all through and as Louis put it: I hear babies cry, I watch them grow, and as Tom wrote: these fragments I have... *etcetera*, but Lord it isn't easy, you see, I have difficulty sleeping, I wake in the dead of night, *You'd drink too if you were in my shoes, I tell you it's enough to drive a man mad*, my mind's diseased, my cranium seethes, much to my surprise I found myself reading *War and Peace*, the first couple of books seemed like a swamp of domestic details, the opening and shutting of a door had to be described every time a character entered or left a room, the second half was quite different, far superior, the act of a madman or drunkard – yes, I recognised it and see now how the tenth chapter of *Under the Volcano* mocks the concept of free will – I enquired about assets and the Index to Probates at Somerset House informed me that Lowry left £11,018 17s. 6d., I slept alone, the days passed, I discovered that in the first edition of Marlowe's translation of Ovid the phrase *white, with incense* appeared as *wives, with incest*, how joyous textual differences can be, how sweet the dissents of scholarship, this book is attributed to X by Y but Y was a fool, it is like his other books but it bears no resemblance to them, Professor Swellhorn provides a conclusive footnote, citing a manuscript, but Dr Borage wants Swellhorn's job and he proves the MS is a forgery, and so we persevere, in icy climes and hot, we hope – fools – that wisdom comes with know-ledge, we growl and drink a lot, we need to master something other than ourselves or our mistresses, and so back to those dust-and-book infested shelves, and now – pay attention, please – a sharp, epic monologue unfolds before an empty theatre, I offer you certain particulars, quite tumultuarily so to speak, oh yes, oh yes yes yes, I rehearse a play that will never be performed and if you want the Célinean dots on the i's – 'It's the brick! ... the brick! ...' – you shall have them... you hear this fellow in the cellarage, Louise, he emits dull ironic laughter, he is the squalid author, peevish under-ground man, *Senex fornicarius!* cackabed! filthy fellow squinting up through the gaps, hoping to catch a glimpse of something private, in thrall to aesthetics and fiction and sensation, fingering his pipe and coughing and getting rid of a recurring dullness, if music be the snack of lust, play on! let's roll! let's take a trip down memory's dark alley and do the twist! let him burble on, telling stories, while the others lie recumbent, yes yes yes, north-by-northwest, four-ways, bedways, let it roll, when he's not playing the voyeur he likes to call attention to himself, here I am! pay attention, look! c'est moi, I'm over here, sat on a Bruegel barrel, by a dead dog's grave crowned with irises, my *Hamlet* in hand, chin resting on my crooked arm, solemn and thoughtful as that bald slim guy on every statue commemorating the double-chinned slippery fat bard, a monologue in an empty theatre, yes, *bong-bong*, who put the dong in ding? aye, answer me that, and while you're at it – and you were always at it, were you not? – fetch me a bright paper party hat, fetch me that hat, do you hear! fetch me a plastic flute and a tin drum, just listen to that racket! he's rapping on the boards with his bloodied knuckles, he's good at getting out of tight spots, aye, and into them also, yes, listen! can you hear what's slightly and slowly uttered, in between the forlorn distant cries of the owl? he's keeping pace with his over-used heart, which bangs miserably on, drama, I'll give you fucking drama, like baldilocks, where theatre is concerned I prefer to play the ghost's part, and only one of us was real, here, pull on my cracker, let's hear it pop honey, *Honey!* read me the joke and pass me the puzzle, bring me a beer and a big tumbler of Bushmills, insatiate cormorant! Coriolanus is dead! fuck the government, I love you! I'll whistle on my way, *I was born under a wandering star...* like Gulliver I have travelled, I believe I can speak with some authority about lutes, laurels, seas of milk and ships of amber, it rained all night the day I left, the weather it was dry, if Bohemia still lies by the sea I'll believe in the sea again, I walked a crooked mile to meet a crooked girl and when I finally got there... she said she'd be on Babylon beach, flying an expensive kite, she said we could walk along by the sea and look for moonstones, but when I got there all I found was her footprints and the tide coming in, don't get cute with me, let's be honest, Smoo Cave smelled of sewage, so did St Anton, oh I had too much to dream last night, a bride drowned in a shower of coloured paper, the words in our conversation became insane twisted butterflies veined with crimson anger, I wrote a list: Robert Burns, Robert Browning, Rupert Brooke, Robert Bridges, Ronald Bottrall, I'm in no joking mood! I may be foggy in the head but, hey, it's time to open up the tired eyes ('I'll buy you a drink some rainy night', 'It's raining now'), yes, oh yes, the man on his knees in Stanley Spencer's *Love Letters* smothers his lover's letters with kisses while she with a strangely ambiguous expression on her face drags envelope after envelope from her breasts, the clock says it's eight after seven, just like in *The Day The Earth Caught Fire*, Louise holds a handful of rain and hey! let's meet up in Montauk! I'll see you at the Memory Motel, please be there, if you want me I'll be in the bar, failing that let's meet up one last time inside the Venus Kebab House, I want nothing from you now, except *that*, because when a man gets too complicated he's unhappy, say do you remember tomorrow? it is the anniversary of that day when we first made love, a cold day today, so cold, paint it black, paint everything black, I could not foresee... she could have been more than a name on the door, *she could have had a very different life but in the end she settled for what was familiar, without risk or danger, their marriage closed over them like a sliding dome, life on the moon, with a machine pumping oxygen, and an eternal vista of craters and sand*, so cold, so very, very cold, 'I told you she was poison'. 'They're all poison sooner or later', I am not a cynic; I am simply an observer – Henry James said that; the kiss originated when the first male reptile licked the first female reptile, implying in a subtle, complimentary way that she was as succulent as the small reptile he had for dinner the night before – F. Scott Fitzgerald: The Notebooks; she had spoken with a kind of brutality which suggested that, whether it is natural or assumed, women have a particular blindness to the feelings of men – Virginia Woolf; the wind had been blowing since 11 o'clock, chasing the dead leaves from one side of the highway to the other – George Eliot; call me a pale egotist, stuffed with deception, a furtive clown, c'est moi, a wrinkled elderly vampire named Ell, *I've seen things you people wouldn't believe...* muddle, muddle, muddle, chimes at midnight, in the old days you could buy a bottle of port for a dollar fifty-five, Alkie, she said (that day in June fell on a Monday), my veins are ancient sluggish rivers clogged with weeds and silt, *I live at night, my vision is painfully acute,* and now I am tottering back to my place, under the sign of the Plough, I am twitching and shattered, the cat sits on the balcony for hours, staring intently at something I can't see, muddle, muddle, muddle, why is *Echoes of Celandine* out of print? a scandal, it sounds worth a look, *Deploys highly wrought thriller tactics to X-ray the soul of a man whose cynicism has hardened into an arctic despair,* Hey, did you know that from where I was back then on a clear day you could see Mount Tantalus? while Queen Victoria, lips held tightly together, glared down at me with venom from her stained plinth, well I'll be damned! – *most of us are* – hey, there's a stake through this shrivelled heart but I'm not dead yet, no, ma'am, exclamation, *shake me up, Judy!* yes, oh yes, I said to her: 'You get around – and your timing's good,' she said to me 'Oh, you *are* a one, Mr L, reely there's no 'olding you once your passions are aflame,' and then she left me at the silent time when the moon had ceased to climb, she left me and I stayed alone thinking over every tone, she did, yes, yet this miserable heart still squirts, this ripped heart greasy and lumpy as chicken giblets is still capable of the occasional miserable throb, tsk, tsk, tsk, take this, an ancient wrinkled copy, *Briefing for a Descent into Hell*, how little we know of the people we sleep with Louise... like Louise always says... *Donna folle! indarno gridi; chi son io tu non saprai*, reading *Women in Love* recently I was puzzled as to what happened to Ursula in between Skrebensky and Birkin, the novel D. H. Lawrence never wrote, also I do not know the colour of the leaves in Oregon today, I know only that today there are many household tasks to be performed, the vacuum cleaner stands to attention – erect, you might say – waiting for action, that is the marvellous thing about a house, there is always something which needs repainting or to be washed or swept up, *All characters in this publication are fictitious and any resemblance to real persons, living or dead, is purely coincidental*, when an author puts that sign up on the gate to the house you know the bastard is lying, abominable reader who reads these lines, do more than read these lines, it is not enough to read between the lines, you must read *behind* the lines, all my characters are authentic, any resemblance to real persons is completely intentional, but they are now all dead, and the dead cannot consult a lawyer, or register a complaint, or write a novel, or give a retaliatory interview, they're out of the game, the living as Jan Gabrial knew get the last word, do you read me, really, question mark, *Force yourself to make friends among people your own age, date girls, and refuse to give in to your tendency to be attracted to older women, it won't be easy, it will often mean you will cry into your pillow, but you can do it, and will be able to look back in years to come and be deeply glad that you made yourself grow up*, the Monday Problems Page, *The Sun*, yes, all that blighted fall the Loch Ness Monster was advertising whisky on the panels beside the escalators at Waterloo, I was reading Hugo von Hofmannsthal, who wrote:

*What is man that he should make plans! I toyed with schemes, but each one, bloated with a drop of my blood, dances before me like a weary gnat against a sombre wall whereon the bright sun of halycon days no longer lies*, and there on the cover of *The Penguin Book of Love Poetry* was a detail from Bronzino's masterpiece, with the naked young male embracing the naked older woman, his long slender fingers around her small left breast, her nipple protruding, engorged, I remembered that day we spent on Skye, we walked all day across a lunar plain, a plain of rock, boulders, mouldering brochs, we came to black lochans and a broken shoreline, at the edge of a cliff we found a heap of stony remains, half under bramble, some fool had chalked on the remains of a shattered wall *Thig crioch air an tl saoghal ach máiridh gaol is cèol*, curious, I wrote these words down, then we went down to the beach and stripped off and splashed in the black ice-cold water, we sat naked under the sun, drying our skin, we laid our coats in the grass and made love, while the seagulls wheeled nearby, screeching, water droplets on her breasts were like shining pearls, my style glows, her black eyes beseeched me: be with me forever, we were in Mills & Boon country, back at the hotel I asked the barman if there was anyone who could translate Gaelic, he was a big, bearded man who wore a kilt, he smiled and said in a thickly accented voice: Aye, that there is, and lawks-a-mercy! it was, ye ken, himself, I wrote down what he said, although it was memorable enough: *The world will end, but love and music go on*, the strains of a polonaise linger in the air, a child howls, a dog barks, a sparrow lands on a rock, Milena's father hops up the grass slope at Theresienstadt, hearing the rifle shots, a spurt of blood spatters his shirt just like Rachel Weisz in *The Favourite*, the man beside him is thrown forwards, he does not move again, I am so very tired of history, her father said, a plangent crash of chords, the Soviet army advances down the ruined street, her mother puts a sign in the window: *Juden*, hoping that she and her daughter will be spared rape, a tank commander lodged in the house, he has a chauffeur who lodges with you, too, please, Milena's mother says to the soldier who is the chauffeur, do not let him touch my daughter, Milena is seventeen years old, the soldier is weary, I can do nothing, he says, he is my commander, but the tank commander is not a rapist, he leaves Milena alone, I have a dream of Canada, her father said, Milena took me to see his grave at Mountain View cemetery, his name was Gustav, his dates are 1894-1965, so long ago now, and as Nelson Algren once bitterly wrote: *After dinner some stiff is certain to ask – in the tone of a bondsman recognising a bail-jumper – 'Well! What are you up to **now**? What's **next**?'* and I remembered the book she'd described to me on that last day in St Anton, so I bought a copy of Max Frisch's *Homo Faber*, I wondered if it would contain any clues, the main character, Walter Faber, is forty-nine years old, the same age as Milena, and he has a brief sexual relationship with a twenty-year-old girl he meets by chance on his travels, she turns out to be his daughter, inadvertent incest, a destructive relationship which ends in death, the book is puzzling yet somehow compelling, the narrative style is oddly feverish and fractured, there's an emphasis on sunlight, heat, intensity, the hero sweats a lot, the only other novel I can think of which I'd also characterise as *feverish* is *Nineteen Eighty-Four*, another book in which the hero enjoys a brief, intense relationship with a much younger woman, another book about deception, betrayal, death and memory, Orwell haunted by his experiences in Catalonia and, earlier than that, in sleepy Southwold, those furtive assignations with Eleanor Jaques of Four Ways, Reydon, that unforgettable summer's day he lured her up Lodge Lane and fucked her in the woods beyond Walberswick, Newdelight the wood was called, above this wood, in The War, JFK's older brother died in a massive explosion, there was scattered wreckage lying there in the undergrowth for twenty or thirty years afterwards, there is an air crash near the start of *Homo Faber*, I wondered if this was one of those stories which turn out to be the fantasies of someone who is dying, it's not, decades later I discovered that in 1974 Max Frisch had travelled to North America and enjoyed a very brief affair with a much younger woman, in the white heat of the aftermath of that experience Frisch wrote *Montauk*, which was published by Suhrkamp Verlag in 1975 and in an English translation by Geoffrey Skelton in 1976, *Montauk, Eine Erzählung*, a story, yes, and what is a novel? a novel is *Montauk*, it is *By Grand Central Station I Sat Down and Wept*, it is *Under the Volcano*, it is *The End of the Affair*, it is *The Life and Opinions of Tristram Shandy, Gentleman*, it is anything by Charles Mergendahl or Greg Hamilton or even (lawks!) rumpy-pumpy Penelope Ashe... on BBC Radio Four there is an adaptation of *Under the Volcano*, the cast list in *Radio Times* includes a character named Everard, is my memory perishing, at fault, blocking out all knowledge of the Consul's long-lost father Everard who, rich, smiling, and moderately sober, leads his son away from the clutches of that faithless Yankee bitch and takes him back to Kashmir to join the family business, manufacturing gas-powered prayer-wheels, or is he, perhaps, the well known brewer of that name? if there are answers they lie in a cupboard blocked by a table, excuse me while I move around some furniture, I am easily confused by authority, Douglas Day in his biography says on his ninety-eighth page that Lowry went to Germany in December 1928 returning on page one-hundred-and-one in the late Spring of 1928, the novelist's powers as a time-traveller have been shockingly neglected, I must be on my way, the fate of every novelist faced by the stump of an incomplete tale, so long, time flies, others are left to live beyond the end, Laura (bless her) went to visit Margerie on a sunny afternoon in January, the widow was by this time living in an apartment which was one of three in a lovely old black-shuttered home in a nice but not pretentious area of Beverly Hills, my first impression of her as she opened the door wrote Laura was one of poised dignity, her apartment had the faint faded mustiness I associate with my grand-mother's house with lace doilies on the arms and backs of overstuffed chairs, Laura afterwards recalled vividly the widow's soft beauty, her poised businesslike manner and those stars in her eyes as she sat talking of Malcolm, Margerie did not like Douglas Day's biography, his image of Malcolm was false, Malcolm wasn't sloppy you know, on the contrary he used to change his shirt *every day*, would you label him a genius asked Laura, a piercing question, there was a deep deep prospectively Conradian silence as the brooding widow thought about it and then at last quietly answered: Yes; and now it is the merry merry month of May in the year following Laura's trip to Beverly Hills (where are you now, Laura?) and I am watching *Dead of Night*, a strange impressive film, suddenly six words in *Gabriola*'s Chapter 28 – room for one more inside mister! – make perfect sense, the bracketed interpolation occurring during the scene where the Greyhound bus enters Nanaimo on Victoria Island and follows a funeral procession consisting of a hearse and five black cars at which moment Ethan overhears a conversation between two men in the seat in front, one an old man with impish features whose words Lowry's Lowryesque protagonist decides in some mysterious way hold a secondary meaning, perhaps many meanings, intended for his ears alone, the old man's memory of trimming coach wheels with vermilion triggering the thought in Ethan that the old man must surely be recalling the funeral hearses of old drawn by stately horses tossing their funeral plumes, *A profound examination of the meaning of human existence,* **October Ferry to Gabriola** *is also a touching love story – a love story that will last!* wrote someone in the publicity department of The New American Library, Inc., laying this syrup on a bed of mixed fruit: *a literary feast* said leading critical journal PLAYBOY, *an intimate novel, its spirit runs deep* thought SATURDAY REVIEW, *Malcolm Lowry's valedictory trembles with the resonance of an original sensibility* asserted THE NATION, paratext is all too often neglected thought L for whom a book jacket was often the best part of modern fiction and usually superior to that first page of porous prose, in *Dead of Night* a bedside clock stops at 4.15am and a man in hospital – a racing car driver recovering from a crash – looks out of the window puzzled by the clock because it is not yet midnight and he has his bedside light on and when he pulls back the curtains he discovers it's daylight outside, a hearse pulled by horses is waiting just below drenched in sunlight, the driver of the hearse looks up at the man and shouts Room for one more inside! when the man has recovered he goes to catch the bus home, someone in the bus queue asks him the time, he realises it's exactly the time when the clock stopped in the hospital, at that moment the bus arrives, the conductor leans out and cries Room for one more inside! the man is stunned to see it's the man who was driving the hearse, he jumps back from the bus in horror, the conductor looks perplexed, the bus pulls away and before it has reached the end of the street the bus driver swerves to avoid a petrol tanker which bursts out of a side street and the double-decker plunges over a steep high railway embankment with what will plainly be catastrophic consequences, an uncanny and disturbing episode, returning from seeing the film I found a letter waiting for me, the crop circle enigma is far from being solved my father writes, still joyously deranged; Smorg says: I am writing an article for the *Circular* newsletter pointing out that the so-called 'Big Bang' never happened (it happened for me father dear – but Smorg would never understand), returning from the film I was anxious to write down what the hearse driver/conductor had actually said, because Lowry had misremembered, had misquoted, how the line of dialogue actually went was: *Just room for one inside, sir*, still it was easy to understand why Lowry was so affected by the movie, it remains an impressive production and very creepy, Lowry's interest was strengthened by it featuring his old acquaintance Michael Redgrave, what struck me much more viewing it again on DVD many years later was the thudding resemblance of the sceptical psychiatric doctor Dr Van Straaten to Waclaw Slabczynski, five chapters later Lowry's character Ethan arrives at the deserted dock where an empty ferry waits and wonders Had he experienced it before? stood right here many times before, wondering: would the Gabriola ferry perhaps not sail at all, was it a nightmare from which he woke in a cold sweat and which was never finished? another invocation of *Dead of Night* which begins with an architect arriving at a rural house and experiencing an acute sense of déjà vu, telling the house occupants they have all been in his dream, some of whose occupants also tell of uncanny and inexplicable experiences, one of which ends in a terrifying nightmare from which the architect wakes to tell his wife he's had the dream again, and then he remembers he has to drive to the country to look at a house, the film ending as it began with his arrival, a cyclical structure of obvious interest to the author of *Under the Volcano*, the years passed, Smorg died, my mother also died, I went to North Farm House to bury them, to clear out the family home, preparatory to selling it, room by room I returned it to its original emptiness, beds, armchairs, the sofa, they all had to go, plus the rickety bookstands built by Smorg to hold his collection of tales of alien abduction, flying saucers of Latin America, ghosts, the secret power of the pyramids, ESP, tracts by a fat smiling Californian fraud named Bubba John, trash for the Red Cross charity shop in the next town, clocks, cutlery, cups, jackets, shoes, a walking stick, my mother's magnifying glass, which she used to read the last detective fiction she'd ever consume, it was playing with this last item that shed new light on an ancient artefact, when I finally turned my attention to the last room of all, my own bedroom, I noticed it for the very first time, examining with that very magnifying glass the painting 'Cougars, With Explorer' I saw that on the satchel slung over the explorer's shoulder were the tiny initials R. F. B., it didn't take long – bless you, Google – to work out the identity of the explorer, those initials, combined with the incongruous Arab headgear, gave the game away, the solitary moustachio'd figure in a desert landscape was plainly Sir Richard Francis Burton – explorer, soldier, translator, polymath – you may recall, Louise (you probably don't, how could you?) that in the first chapter, or what was once the first chapter before the chapters were abolished and the first half of the manuscript with it, I identified the painter of this preposterous scene as either an ignoramus or a tease, plainly the last option is now definitive, our hack painter had a sense of humour, Sir Richard Francis Burton – I must visit his extraordinary grave – was tremendously risqué, there was the heroic aspect to be admired, of course, an adventurer of the sort to which the adjective *swashbuckling* attaches itself with wearying predictably, a master of disguise, a man who ventured into forbidden regions of Arabia and the mysterious interior of the Horn of Africa, an author with the temperament of an encyclopaedist, writer, translator and editor of some forty volumes, like Lowry's hero Geoffrey Firmin he was appointed a British consul, and like Firmin he ended up in remote exotic locations – Fernando Po, Brazil, Damascus, and, finally, Trieste, where he died on 20 October 1890 (on this day, fourteen years later, at the main railway station in Trieste, an impoverished wannabe writer called James Joyce rocked up with his wife Nora, so it goes), risqué? why (I hear you ask) – why was the unknown painter of the lurid daub on my bedroom wall so discreet in identifying his hero? easy-peasy, because of his notoriety as the translator and editor of *The Kama Sutra* (1883), *The Book of the Thousand Nights and a Night* (10 vols., 1885-1888) and *The Perfumed Garden* (1886), scandalous books about the ever-interesting topic of human sexual behaviour in all its sparkling and greasy forms, R. F. B. discovered that sex sold, I struggled for forty-seven years, he said, I never had a compliment nor a Thank You nor a single farthing, I translated a doubtful book in my old age and immediately made sixteen thousand guineas, now that I know the tastes of England, he told his wife, we need never be without money, glad that's sorted, and now 'Cougars, With Explorer' can go into the skip, along with 'Lioness, With Her Cubs' and all the other junk, our possessions mean little or nothing to others, people die and life goes on and inside that banal truth lies an ocean of pain, Milena, Milena, like Vronsky, I had to go on, I went to Africa (like R. F. B.) but that is quite another story, as for this one, I suppose I should point out that all the events described had occurred by the time I was twenty-eight years old, a mere fraction of that piled-up assemblage of years and experiences which we call a life, *Leftover Life to Kill*, another good title, Is there a crown of thorns over your heart, question mark, a spike has gone deep enough into mine, time changes the places that knew us, and if we go back in after years, still even then it is not the old spot; the gate swings differently, new thatch has been put on the old gables, the road has been widened, and the sward the driven sheep lingered on is gone, who dares to think then, question mark, for faces fade as flowers, and there is no consolation, Richard Jefferies, 'Wild Flowers' (1885), yes, years passed, so many people that I knew have gone into the dark, Ivan Berg, D'eath, Marty, Bridget, Jane, unwritten footnotes to this tale, and day followed day, year year, and certain things became clearer, Penelope Ashe, author of steamy *Naked Came The Stranger*, never existed, she was no less than twenty-four people – a bunch of *Newsday* journalists led by Mike McGrady, who set out to satirise sex-stuffed bestsellers like *Valley of the Dolls* and *The Carpetbaggers* by producing a sex novel which was, so to speak, tongue in cheek and utterly devoid of any literary substance, naturally it sold... enough! everything's been returned which was owed and I must now take up some of the ragged ends which I have left behind me and lay them before you no matter how odd soever your brains be, the fact is I've never been back to most of the places I've mentioned, everything changes, Edward Thomas finished with: *I shall not forget her 'Go now'* but later returned and in pencil wrote a further four lines, beginning: *Those two words shut a door*, so it goes, Oregon and Washington State are blank as the snow on the mountain tops, the same is true for St Anton, and on the occasions when I have returned it's been a shock, just as it was a shock many years later to stand in front of Georges Merle's *L'Envoûteuse* in an air-conditioned gallery and find myself staring at a replica of my darling Milena, I do declare it gave me quite a turn, it sent me into a spin, afterwards I needed a beer, many beers, and so the years go by, go by, go by, I went back to Vancouver just once, quite recently, downtown it seemed like a different city to the one I'd known half a century earlier, I didn't recognise any of the tall glass buildings, I was there less than a day, I took a taxi to Mountain View cemetery, it lies west of Fraser Street and extends for twelve blocks, the graves are identified according to Section, Range, Block, Plot and Lot, while I was there I looked up H. L. Maddox in the telephone directory, she wasn't listed, I tried an internet search, there was an H. L. Maddox who lived alone on Vancouver Island, but it probably wasn't her, I looked at the address on Google StreetView, it showed a one-storey house – a bungalow really – which looked in a poor state, with an unkempt garden, no, please, this cannot be my Honey, by now, surely, she's a plump white-haired rosy-cheeked grandmother, the widow of a wealthy man, in a split-level house overlooking English Bay, grown-up sons, fertile daughters, three dogs and two cats, and a glossy tortoise with a head like the tip of an old leathery penis, which she has whimsically named Ell, whereas Milena was easier to find, she was in the Masonic section, not far from her parents, the assistant in the office reminded me that the Masonic section no longer has anything at all to with Masons, I nodded gravely as one should in such a place, he gave me a map and pointed out the direction to take, it took ten minutes to find her, as I walked down the long avenues between the blocks the noise of traffic on Fraser gradually dropped away, it was a beautiful day with just a few fluffy white clouds scudding across a pure blue sky, did I say scudding? how easily one drops into syrup, when I found it I was surprised by how small and simple the grave was, just a small rectangular stone set flat into the surrounding grass, the grass needed cutting, it was a little unkempt, I pulled up a weed but there wasn't much else I could do without a pair of shears, I'd brought along a single red rose, I laid it on the stone, it bore her name and the year of her birth, the year of her death, nothing more, Militká Slabczynski, I can't write about how I felt to be looking at her grave, I stared at it for a long time and then I convulsed and shook until finally I walked away with wet cheeks, I needed violins in the background but all I heard was motor vehicles, I went back to my hotel, well that's it folks that's it (as Nina Simone once sang), the next day I flew to Winnipeg, I had business there with Young Logistical Solutions Inc., none of this is true obvs, it just sounds better than what really happened, because do you remember tomorrow? I do, all the time, the world had moved on and on, as the world always does, yes, you see – remember – it was poor Jan Gabrial who unwittingly wrote, *do you remember tomorrow?* and as P. K. Dick (who was sharper) wrote: *Much had happened in the next year*, besides 2307 West 41st Street was demolished long before I ever went back, the entire apartment block was removed for retail development, today there's an organic produce store where the driveway to Alicia's apartment once existed, everything has changed, everywhere, that Scottish city which featured in the original and now deleted draft is today a traffic-choked parody of its old self, the Tartan Tower was demolished years ago (or in this fiction just a day or so ago), The Woolpack in Keswick is no longer a pub, likewise The King of Bohemia closed, today it's a clothes shop, The Bridge Motel was torn down, everything has changed, everywhere, which is why I live alone now, in a great silence, I am old, very old, I am one hundred years old today, cheers! happy birthday to me! the fact is I can barely move and when I do I squeak, I need oiling, pass me the Nivea Creme and some Southern Comfort, you see, it is like this, the fire is out and spent the warmth thereof, I am living inside the ruins of a life, it bears some resemblance to the remains of Castle Acre Priory in quiet Norfolk, all the windows have gone, the flint walls are melted down by time and rain, nothing will ever happen here again, and now, finally, I inhabit a house without the distraction of a single flickering screen, no TV, no smartphone, no laptop or tablet, only tablets very small and mostly white, like Gulliver I have retreated from humanity, in my case it's to a small whitewashed house on a mountainside, I am not saying where it is, you might want to come and see me, I detest visitors, I am neither a guru with a store of nuggets of wisdom nor a dribbler of quaint reminiscences for an eager young archivist or biographer, I no longer need people, sing no sad songs, I am beyond sex and companionship, leave me be, leave me be, let go of me, suppose you keep your secrets and I'll keep mine, I am happy as I am, I listen to music, I read books, I sleep, I walk as far as a small lake, go round it, and then return, the only living beings I meet are sheep, very occasionally I see the shepherdess, a strapping wench, rosy-cheeked with long auburn hair, how I abhor the sight of her, she is probably the type who writes what she believes to be poetry, when I spot her afar off I dip down out of sight behind a drystone wall, I wait until she's gone, she came to the door a few times when I first retreated here, I pretended to be out, in the end she gave up, I have a view of rock, nothing but wonderful rock, rock with a fiery history which is now rested, plus a sky which is mainly empty and grey, or some days layered with dark cloud, a prospect of desolation, it rains a lot, I like it here, not true, not really, I am lying, I am for instance sick of books, like Edgar Fripp I turn away with curled lip and downturned mouth from a mass of fictitious nonsense, sufficient to say I am exhausted, quite worn out, my vision dulled, my body stiff and cold, my temperature too high, my spirits too low, my brow and brain feverish, the night plays tricks, I crunch a dozen paracetamol, the ache remains, my energy levels are low, too low, my voice has dropped to a whisper, my hand shakes, my handwriting is as spidery as any half-blind geriatric's, whisper that our revels now are ended, the people all are gone, the party's over, the sword has outworn its sheath, the actors and actresses are virtually dead, those members of the cast who still endure are in a twilight zone of illness and medication, our teeth and skin and bladders and hips are not what they were, it's so hard to get on, we sag, we bruise easily, bones and solids not what they were, must get some rest, fetch ampules, fetch water, tissues, a syringe, some camphorated oil, some shots of morphine, a spoonful of honey, a towel and a mop, a thermometer, in pharmacies we are greeted as valuable customers, packages of this and that await us, the shelves are loaded and fast replenished, tablets, supplements, ointments, bandages, and small dark packets of pads discreetly labelled *Drips and Dribbles*, yes, ghosts go along with us until the windy, leaky end and what will survive of us is mainly old stained paperbacks, they will turn up in cluttered second-hand book shops or on trestle tables in High Streets where rigid volunteers stand to collect for A Good Cause, fools, thumb through the boxes, what have we here? *The Penguin Book of English Verse* and just inside: *L*, the ink identifying a year quite faded and the price in pencil: *£1*, six for a fiver, look at some more, *Tinker, Tailor, Soldier, Spy* in the Bantam paperback edition and inside: *April 26, Skykomish, E. Sharp*, leave it alone, let it be, have done with you, walk on, drive away, as I did, quite recently, never absolutely free of the fierce suck and tug of nostalgia, I left my fabulous fictive isolated home and went on a long journey, back to where this all began, England, I hadn't been there for decades, I'm an exile on main street, the roads everywhere have changed, where there was once farmland there was now a dual carriageway, the chalk hillside had been cut open to permit the passage of a motorway, the hills were alive with the sound of motor vehicles, a shower of particulates and drifts of diesel fumes floated across the wilted hedgerows where no birds sang, what butterflies there were to be seen lay on the ground choking and flapping their tired chequered wings in a last rictus of defiance, I made that up of course, truth is I wasn't able to get as far as the old family home, lately the weather had been acting strangely, there'd been heavy rainfall for a week and, to my astonishment, the old road where I had played as a child was partly flooded, the far end of the street was under water, I could see it covering our old front lawn and the concrete drive, water reached up the brick wall under my old bedroom window, water darkened the brickwork below my parents' bedroom, where I had stood and watched a woman walk out of my life, a woman who only existed in the first draft, I stared at an actually existing scene for a few minutes, then I went back to my car and drove away, a wooden door is closed, it's all over now Bub, my pen is stubbed, my paper spent, my ink wasted, my wits gravelled, it is now publique, and so brazenly to conclude: I have a soundtrack to my life and I play it from time to time, on that day – there were plenty more but a one-hundred-year-old man's song lists soon become boring – Roberta Flack sang 'Our Ages or Our Hearts' and Tom Paxton sang 'I've Got Nothing But Time' and Bob Dylan sang 'This Wheel's on Fire' and the Stones belted out 'Memory Motel' and Art Garfunkel crooned 'Woyaya' and then Anjani Thomas and Leonard Cohen dueted 'Never Got to Love You' followed by Lucinda Williams singing 'Everything Has Changed', it was late April you see and the white blossom which lined the country lanes of Hampshire reminded me of another April day long ago, when at a gas station in snowbound Washington State I stayed in the car and watched as Milena walked across the forecourt to pay, a Red Setter slumbered on the warm concrete and as she passed by she stooped and patted it, the dog yelped with pleasure and wagged its tail, while this was going on a long chunk of snow as big as a person broke free and slid down the corrugated roof to smash softly in a broken heap behind her, she didn't hear it or notice it, she paid for the fuel and came back, Is everything okay? she asked, she said she thought I looked sad, No, everything's fine, I replied, and then we drove on, into what little future we two had left, and on and on, into what happened next and what happened after that, and what occurred in all the time that followed, *bong-bong*.